THE MAYOR'S SON

BY

SUSAN L. PARE'

MORE BOOKS BY THIS AUTHOR

Willerton Woods

Cowtown

Floating Face Down
A Sheriff "Cowboy" Berkson Mystery Novel – Book Three

Let's Play Autopsy

A Bad Week In Hollister
A Sheriff "Cowboy" Berkson Mystery Novel – Book Two

Don't Smother Your Mother
A Sheriff "Cowboy" Berkson Mystery Novel – Book One

Crossing Sydney

Table of Contents

THE MAYOR'S SON

For Jacquie

Chapter One

"Dad, stop the car!" Leslie screamed.

Augie Austin hit the brakes, bringing the car to a sudden stop, throwing everyone in the car forward. "What the hell, Leslie," he shouted. "You scared the shit out of me."

"Look, Dad, over there," Leslie cried out. "There's someone under the popcorn wagon."

Austin glanced over to his right. "Ah, shit," he said. "It looks like a woman. Everyone stay in the car."

He opened his car door, got out, and walked over to get a better look at the body that was under the wagon. He bent down so he could see the woman's face and he wished he hadn't eaten breakfast. He fought to hold back the vomit that was rising in his throat. There was no doubt that the person was dead.

"Who is it, dear?" Mrs. Austin asked as she rolled down her car window.

"Leslie," Mr. Austin called to his daughter, ignoring his wife's question.

"What?" Leslie responded.

"Run down to the police station and tell Pete to get up here."

"But I have heels on. I can't run in my heels."

"Then walk. Just go get him."

Leslie sighed. "Do I have to?"

"I'll go, Dad," Tommy, Leslie's younger brother, yelled to his dad from the back seat of the car.

"Fine. You go get him. Tell him to get up here right now."

"Be careful crossing the street," his mother said.

1

"Mom, I'm ten. I know how to cross streets," Tommy told her as he got out of the car and started running to the police station.

"Why didn't you go?" Mrs. Austin asked her husband. "You know I don't like Tommy crossing the street by himself."

"Because I have to make sure no one disturbs anything, that's why. And, don't you think it's about time you quit babying him?"

Mrs. Austin gave her husband 'the look', turned her face away, and rolled up her car window.

Pete Drollstrom, one of Columbus' three full-time police officers, was asleep at his desk. He jumped, almost falling off his chair, as Tommy ran through the door yelling his name.

Drollstrom started to reach for his handgun. Then, brought his hand back up when he remembered his service pistol was locked up in the safe.

"Pete, dad wants you to come quick," Tommy yelled. "We just found a dead person."

Pete stared at him. "What did you say?"

"We were driving to church and we found a dead woman lying in the street."

"Where at?"

"Up at 4 corners. It's under old man Hermann's popcorn wagon."

"Where the hell are my keys?" he muttered to himself, as he stood up. He glanced over at Tommy. "Go tell your dad I'll be right there.

"It's only a block away. You don't need to drive," Tommy told him.

"Go on now," Pete ordered.

Tommy stayed where he was, watching Officer Drollstrom open and close the drawers to his desk, looking for the keys to his police vehicle.

"Got 'em," Pete yelled and ran past Tommy and out the door.

Tommy ran after him shouting, "Can I ride with you in the police car?"

"No way. I'm on official police business. I can't have a civilian riding with me."

"A what?" Tommy asked.

"A civilian. A person who isn't a cop. You're not a cop, so that makes you a civilian."

"Oh," Tommy replied.

Tommy watched as Officer Drollstrom jumped into the squad car and sped down the street, lights flashing and sirens blaring. In less than ten seconds, Drollstrom had parked behind Austin's car and was out of the squad car.

Tommy kicked a small stone off the sidewalk into the street and started walking back to his father's car. He glanced up the street at Officer Drollstrom and mumbled, "What a dick head."

Pete exited the police car and walked over to Chief Austin, who was standing next to the body. He looked down at the young woman. "Do you know who she is?"

"I do."

"How can you tell? Her face is a mess. Man, somebody really did a job on her, didn't they?"

Chief Austin looked at Officer Drollstrom with

disgust. "Keep your voice down. My family is sitting right there listening to everything we say. Show a little respect, will you?"

"What did I say that was disrespectful?" Drollstrom asked, defensively. "Maybe, you should move your car so they can't hear us."

"Can the attitude, Pete."

"Or, what? You gonna fire me? Oh, ya, that's right. You can't."

Chief Austin backed a few steps away from Officer Drollstrom and took a deep breath, attempting to calm himself. He walked over to his car, got in, and pulled away from the crime scene. Ignoring the red stop light, he pulled around the corner onto Ludington Street and parked in front of Sharrow's Drug Store.

"You go on ahead to church," he told his wife. "I'm going to be tied up here for a while."

"Where's Tommy?" Catherine asked him.

"He's on his way. Circle round the block and pick him up."

"Do you know who the girl is?" his wife asked him.

"I do, but I'll need a positive ID before I can say for sure."

"Who is it, Augie?"

Chief Austin shook his head no. "I can't tell you, Catherine. Not now."

Chief Austin watched his wife pull away from the curb. As he walked back around the corner, he saw Pete trying to pull the woman out from under the wagon. "What the hell are you doing?" he screamed at

4

him.

Pete jumped back, letting go of the girl's arms. "Crap, you scared me," he exclaimed.

"Pete, what do you think you're doing?" Austin asked again. "You know you can't be touching her. What the hell were you thinking?"

"I just wanted to get her out from under the wagon and cover her up before anyone saw her. What's the big deal anyway?"

"Step away from her, Pete. Get the tape out of the car and start securing this area."

Pete stared at him, not moving. "I don't remember that being in my job description," he said, smirking.

Chief Austin stared back at Pete, stepped back a few feet, slowly pulled his gun out of his holster, and aimed it at Pete.

Pete's face turned white; fear written in his eyes. "What do you think you're doing?" he asked Austin. "You know better than to aim a loaded gun at someone."

"I do know that," Austin said softly. "Unless, of course, you intend to use it."

"You're bluffing. There's no way you're gonna shoot me. Now, put that gun away or I'll have my dad fire your ass," Pete stared up at Austin. "This isn't funny, Augie."

"That's Chief Austin to you. And, you're right. It isn't funny," Austin said, as he pulled the trigger.

"I've got a better idea," Austin said. "You go back

to the office and call the medical examiner. Tell him to get down here asap. I'll put up the crime scene tape. Got it?"

"Got it," Pete muttered. "That's Jerry Severson, right?" he asked.

"Right."

"You know it's gonna take him some time to get here, don't you?"

"I'm aware of that fact," Austin replied.

Pete started walking towards the squad car.

"Leave the car here, Pete," Chief Austin said.

Pete glanced at Chief Austin. "You want me to walk?" Pete said, indignantly.

"Leave the car here. I need it," Austin said again.

Pete gave him a dirty look, turned around, and started walking the block back to the police station.

As Chief Austin watched Pete waddle down the sidewalk, heading towards the police station, he shook his head and muttered, "What a dick head."

Chapter Two

Dr. Jerry Severson, the medical examiner for Columbia County, made it from Portage to Columbus in record time. He loved his new 1957 Ford Fairlane. It was fast and powerful and when he turned on the flashing lights and siren, which had been provided by the county, he was king of the road. Plus, it was definitely a chick magnet.

He came to a screeching stop and looked for a place to park. West James Street was taped off, so turning that way wasn't an option. He decided to leave his car where it was. He put it in park and got out.

Chief Austin was leaning on his squad car, a container of coffee in his hand, talking to Deputy Jacquie Gorski. He glanced over at Severson, gave him a wave, and watched him as he crossed the street.

"You got here awful fast, Jerry. You got a jet engine in that car of yours?"

"She does move out. No doubt about it. So, what do we have here?"

"It's a local girl. I know who it is, but you have to make a positive identification. There's a lot of trauma to her face. She might have been thrown out of a car and rolled under the wagon or she could have been placed there. I can't tell."

"Is this the way you found her?" the medical examiner asked.

"Not exactly," Chief Austin replied.

"How so?"

"When I found her, she was totally under the wagon. Drollstrom tried to pull her onto the sidewalk. I didn't catch him until it was too late."

"Damn. Now the body's been compromised," exclaimed Severson. "What the hell is wrong with that guy?"

"Damned if I know. I'd give anything to be able to get rid of him."

"Why don't you?" Severson asked as he bent down to take a look at the dead girl.

"Politics."

"Isn't it always?" Severson commented as he started to examine the body. "She's young. Can't be more than twenty or so."

"She just turned twenty-one," Austin told him. "I went to the birthday party her parents threw for her at Club 60."

Chief Austin and his deputy watched as Dr. Severson checked out the body and bagged her hands and feet.

After a few minutes, Austin asked, "Any idea how long she's been dead?"

"I'd say eight to twelve hours. Probably died around midnight. I'll know more when I get her on the table. Help me move her to the sidewalk, will you?"

Austin and Severson gently lifted the girl's body and laid it down on a blanket. Severson turned the body on its side and checked for markings on her back. "It looks like she took some kind of a beating," he commented. "Her back has a lot of red welts on it."

"Shit, Jerry. Are you saying she was beaten to death?"

"No. These welts are recent but not deep. They didn't even bleed. I've seen this before."

8

"When?" Austin asked him.

"It was when I was still in private practice. I had a patient whose wife got a little carried away during one of their S&M sessions. She loved whipping him and he loved to be whipped. Only, one night she was pissed at him about something, ignored his safe word, and took it a little too far." He grunted as he knelt down again. "Damn knee," he muttered.

"It still bothers you, does it?" Austin asked.

"Sometimes. Is there a place nearby where I can get a cup of coffee?"

Chief Austin turned to his deputy, who was staring at Dr. Severson. "Jacquie, would you mind running down to Earl's and getting some coffee for Dr. Severson?"

She glanced over at Chief Austin, a blank look on her face. "I'm sorry, Chief. What did you say?"

Austin grinned at her. "Coffee. Earl's. Now."

Jacquie blushed slightly and smiled back at her boss. "Sorry. Do you want another one?"

"Sounds good. Get one for yourself, too. Tell Georgie to put it on my tab."

Chief Austin watched as Severson pulled a thermometer out of the woman's liver, checked the temperature, and made a note of it in his notebook.

"Temperature is about right for being dead around eight to twelve hours. I think the damage to her face could have been caused by being thrown out of a moving car."

"Or, drag marks," Austin added. "Is it possible she was dragged under the wagon?"

"Possibly. Her chest has some damage, too."

9

"Was she molested?"

"It's hard to tell here, but there's some bruising in that area. Again, I'll know more after I do the autopsy."

Austin stayed quiet as the medical examiner gently examined the rest of the woman's body. After a few minutes, Severson stood and stretched out his tall, lean body. He glanced over at Jacquie, who had just arrived with the coffee. "Ah, Jacquie. Good timing."

Jacquie smiled and handed him one of the containers. "Black with one sugar. Right?"

Severson gave her one of his jaw-dropping, heart-stopping smiles. "You remembered." He took a sip and sighed. "Man, that hits the spot. I'm telling you, Augie, you better be good to this girl or I'll steal her away from you."

"You'll have a fight on your hands if you try. Do you have any idea what I had to go through to hire her? It's taken a long time for this town to accept the fact that there's a woman on the police force."

"I can imagine," Severson replied.

"Are you about finished here?" Chief Austin asked, getting back to business.

"I am. Just waiting for the ambulance."

"What do you think was the cause of death?" Austin asked him.

"You'll know when I know, Augie."

"Is it okay to cover her up?" Austin asked.

"By all means, cover her up."

"Jacquie, cover her up, will you?"

Jacquie shook her head in agreement and wrapped the blanket around the young woman's body.

She reached down and gently smoothed the hair back out of the girl's eyes.

"Did you know her?" Austin asked as he noticed tears welling up in Jacquie's eyes.

"We went to school together. She was a few years behind me, but her sister was in my class. She seemed like a nice enough kid."

"She was," Chief Austin agreed.

"Last I heard, her sister was living in Madison," Jacquie told him.

"She still is. She's married and has a little boy."

"This will be hard on the family," Jacquie stated. "They were really close."

"It's always hard on the families, Jacquie. Young or old, good or bad. It's always hard," said Austin. He stopped talking as the noise of the approaching ambulance's siren filled the air.

A half-hour later the ambulance drove off, headed to the morgue where, in a few hours, Dr. Severson would perform an autopsy on the body. He had a name from Chief Austin, but an identification would still need to be made by her parents or a close relative.

Chief Austin decided he needed to inform her parents as soon as possible. News travels fast in a small town like Columbus and he didn't want her parents to hear the news of their daughter's death from someone else. Identifying the body by her parents would just be a formality in this case. He knew, without a doubt, that the dead girl they found was Debbie Nelson. Chief Austin and his wife had been friends with the Nelsons for years and he had watched their two girls grow up. This notification would be one of the hardest in his career.

"Do you want to get some lunch?" Dr. Severson asked him.

Austin looked at him and shook his head no. "Sorry, I want to get over to the Nelsons before they hear about this from someone else. Plus, we have to finish going over every inch of this area before we open the street to the public again."

"How about you, Jacquie? Are you hungry?"

Jacquie looked surprised. "You want to have lunch with me? I don't know if. . .. I mean I'd love to, but. . ."

"What I think Jacquie is trying to tell you, Doc, is that she's on duty and can't make it." He glanced over at his Deputy and grinned. "Isn't that right, Jacquie?"

"Yes. Sorry, Dr. Severson, but I can't. Thanks for asking, though."

Severson gave her the once over and smiled. "That's a shame. Perhaps, some other time. And, please, call me Jerry."

Jacquie stared at him for a few seconds, then, broke eye contact. "Okay, then," she said. "I've got work to do," and walked away.

"You are a piece of work," Austin said. "Is there a woman you won't hit on?"

Severson laughed. "Two. My mother and my sister. As far as I'm concerned, all the rest are fair game."

Chapter Three

Deputy Jacquie Gorski glanced over at her boss; a questioning look on her face.

"What?" Austin asked.

"Shouldn't you be on your way home? Catherine called over an hour ago telling you that dinner was ready."

"Dinner can wait. Right now, all I want is a good stiff drink. How about you?"

"Whataya got hiding in that bottom drawer?" Jacquie asked him.

"Good old Kentucky bourbon. Twelve years old."

"Jim Beam?"

"What else. Do you wanna drink?" Austin asked her.

"Damn right, I do," Jacquie said, grinning.

Austin was just about to remove the bottle of bourbon from the bottom drawer of his desk when Officer Drollstrom entered the room. Drollstrom looked at Jacquie and smiled. "It's after six. Why are you two still here?" he asked her.

"Because, we don't keep banking hours, like some people I know. The better question is – what are you doing here? You never work late," Jacquie replied.

"I think I left my shades here," Pete said, as he walked over to his desk. "Yep, here they are." He put on his sunglasses, pushed them down his nose, and stared at her over the top of the frames. "I'd be sick if I lost these," he said. "They cost a fortune."

"Well, then, it's a good thing you didn't lose them," Jacquie said.

13

"By the way, Chief, did you find out anything else on the Nelson case?" Pete asked as he moved towards the door to leave.

"No. Her parents are taking it pretty hard. It's hard to lose a child."

"Well, at least they have another one to fall back on," Pete said, jokingly.

"You really are a jerk, Pete," Jacquie said, disgusted by his remark.

"What? You can't take a joke?" he said, smirking.

Chief Austin reached behind him, pulled an arrow out of its quiver, and nocked it into the bow string. He carefully eyed his target. Satisfied that he was spot on, he pulled the arrow back and let it go, hitting Drollstrom in his heart, and killing him instantly.

"It's not the time or the place. So, is there anything else you need?" Chief Austin asked him.

"You two seem awful anxious to get rid of me. What's going on? Come on. Tell me."

"Not a damn thing is going on," Jacquie said, raising her voice. "We're tired. We just lost a friend and I can't see that there's any humor in her death. So, just get the hell out of here."

"All right. I'm going." As Drollstrom walked out the door, he muttered, "Bitch!"

Jacquie looked over at Chief Austin and shook her head. "I swear, Chief, one of these days I'm gonna kill him."

"Not today, Jacquie. We've had enough drama

for one day." He reached down and pulled the bottle of bourbon out of the drawer, along with two glasses.

Jacquie watched as he started to pour the amber liquid into a glass. "Make mine a double," she said.

Austin smiled, poured a little extra into her glass, and handed her the drink.

Columbus was a small town with a small-town budget. The town council had decided that it could only afford to hire three full-time police officers but did acknowledge that only three officers could not fill the twenty-four-hour day sufficiently. So, instead of hiring a fourth full-time cop, they had decided it would be more cost-efficient to hire part-time help. It actually cost the town more in the long run, but using the term 'part-time' seemed to placate the few citizens who attended the town council meetings and objected to what they considered excessive expenditures.

Officer Benny Benisch was one of the part-timers who worked nights, from six to midnight. He was on duty and stopped by the station, surprised to see his boss was still working. "You're late for dinner. Catherine is going to be upset," Benisch said.

"It won't be the first time and it certainly won't be the last. This case is going to take up a lot of my time until we get it solved."

"Any idea of what might have happened to Debbie?" Benisch asked.

"None."

"I hear she was naked when you found her," Benisch commented.

"Not quite. She had some of those fancy panties on."

"Fancy panties? What the hell are fancy panties?"

"You know, Benny, the kind that has a string that goes in the ass and just a little patch of cloth to cover the hoohah."

Benny cracked up. "The hoohah? You call it a hoohah? Or, my God, wait until I tell Betty what you just said," he sputtered, laughing so hard he could hardly speak.

Austin watched him, trying to hold back a grin. "You will not tell Betty. Understand?"

Benny glanced at him and continued laughing.

"I mean it, Benny. Got it?"

Benny shook his head yes, reached for his cup of water, and took a small sip. "Yes, Sir, I got it!" he replied. "It just that. . ."

"Enough. You say nothing or I'll fire your ass."

Benny grinned. "Sure, you will. Okay, my lips are sealed."

"They better be. Call if you need me or if anything important comes up tonight."

"Will do," Benny told him.

Chief Austin stood up, grabbed his hat, and headed for the door. "By the way, I changed the combination to the safe. I wrote it down and put it in an envelope in the back of my desk drawer," he told Benisch.

"Okay. Although, I don't see why I should need it. By the way, do you still have Drollstrom's gun locked up?"

"I do and make sure you don't give him the combination," Austin said.

"Are you ever going to give it back to him?"

"I don't know. Maybe, someday."

"My god, Chief, he's a police officer. What if he needs it? What if he gets killed in the line of duty because he couldn't defend himself?"

"Unfortunately, I doubt that will happen. Hell, he was a Marine. He should know how to defend himself. Besides, I know for a fact that he has another gun."

"A hand gun?" Benisch asked.

"Yep. He keeps it in an ankle holster. He doesn't think I know about it."

"He's a real cowboy, isn't he?"

"No, he's not. He is a real idiot, though," Austin replied.

Chapter Four

At seven o'clock that evening, four young women huddled around a table in Fireman's Tavern, talking. Every few seconds one of them looked around to make sure no one was close enough to hear their conversation.

"Say what you will, I'm scared," Annie said. "Debbie was in over her head, doing that S&M shit. We all agreed that we wouldn't do any of that kinky crap with our customers."

"She was warned to stop and she didn't listen. She was bound to get hurt eventually," Rose declared.

"Hell, she liked it," Karen said. "She told me she got off on it."

"Well, good for her. And, look where it got her," Annie stated. "We didn't go into this business to get our rocks off. We did it to make enough money so we could open our own restaurant. This town needs a nice family-oriented place where kids are welcome and that was our goal. She forgot about the big plan and now it's all ruined. Damn her, anyway."

Sandra, the fourth woman at the table, had listened quietly to her three friends who had been carrying on for the past thirty minutes. She took a swallow of her beer and slammed the glass down on the table. "Will you three shut the hell up? Nothing is ruined. There's nothing to tie Debbie to what we've been doing. The only way we could have a problem is if one of you doesn't keep your mouth shut. And, Pat, of course. I'm pretty sure that as long as Pat keeps getting his cut, he won't say anything. Right now, though, I'm not so sure about you three."

"But the police are sure to talk to us. Everyone knows that we were friends with Debbie," Annie said.

"The police are going to talk to everyone, not just us. We have nothing to be concerned about. Our money is safely tucked away. We're good, ladies. So, stop your damn worrying and whining and drink up," Sandra said.

Rose looked up from her glass. "Are we working tonight?" she asked quietly. "I could use the money."

"You are fucking kidding me?" Annie asked her.

"Well, I just thought. . . I don't know. It's still early and I don't have any other plans for tonight."

Sandra smiled at her, bent closer to her, and whispered something in her ear.

"What?" Rose asked her. "I couldn't understand you."

Sandra ignored her.

"Tell me, Sandra. What did you say?" Rose asked again.

"Forget it." Sandra reached for her purse and stood up. "I'm out of here, ladies. Remember what we talked about and I'll see you all Tuesday."

"What are we doing on Tuesday?" Rose asked.

"Are you really that dumb?" Annie asked.

"We work Tuesday night. Remember, Rose? We talked about taking tonight and tomorrow night off," Karen said patiently.

"Sorry. Really, I'm sorry. I just can't get my head around all of this. A couple of nights off will do me some good."

Sandra locked eyes with her. "It better, Rose,

because if you don't get it together, the same thing that happened to Debbie could happen to you."

Rose's face turned red, as her temper rose to the surface. "Don't threaten me, you bitch," she whispered, angrily. "I'm not Debbie and I don't do the sick crap that she did."

"Just saying, is all," Sandra told her. She sighed and sat back down in her chair. "I'm sorry, Rose. This has affected all of us and we all need to chill. Debbie's death wasn't our fault. It was hers. She didn't stick to the rules and it got her killed. Let's get past this and move on. Okay?"

"Fine with me," Rose said. "I'm sorry I called you a bitch."

"And, I'm sorry I snapped at you. Remember, ladies, the next few days are going to be hard, but we have to act normal. Got it?" Sandra told them.

Sandra's three friends nodded in agreement.

"You know our income is going to be down by a fifth," Karen commented. "That's going to put us even further behind our goal. Do you think we should consider recruiting another girl? Maybe, this time, it could be someone from out of town."

Annie shrugged and looked at Sandra. "What do you think?" she asked Sandra.

"You first. Tell me what do you think?"

"I'm not sure that's a good idea," Annie said. "We're playing with fire now. Do we want to take that risk?"

"You're right," Karen agreed. "It was a bad idea."

"Rose?" Sandra asked.

"I don't know. Whatever you guys decide to do,

I'm good with."

"Then, it's a no," Sandra told them. "We're just going to have to work a little harder to take up the slack. Maybe, we could ask Pat to add an hour a night to the schedule. We work five nights a week, so that would be an extra twenty hours, which gives us the same number of hours that we were doing with Debbie."

"I'm good with that," Annie said. "You want to add an hour to the end of the shift or the beginning?"

"I think the end. Seven is a little early for a booty call for a lot of guys. I think we should go to one a.m."

"Fine with me," Karen told her.

"Rose?" Sandra said. "You want to add anything?"

"Nope. Eight to one it is."

"Okay, then," Sandra said, smiling. "I'm out of here. Take care."

As Sandra walked away from the table, and out the tavern door, Rose muttered, "Who died and made that bitch boss?"

Matt Leyson was off duty and enjoying his third beer of the evening. It would be his last drink of the evening, as he was scheduled to be at work at four the next morning. He needed to get home soon and go to bed.

He was sitting on a stool with his back to the bar, drink in hand, watching the four women in the next room. He wondered what they were talking about. At one point they raised their voices and it looked like a fight was about to erupt. Then, the Peary woman sat back down, said something, and it seemed that whatever the problem had been was gone.

Matt turned back to the bar, thinking about having one more beer before he left. As he glanced up at the mirror behind the bar, he caught Sandra Peary's reflection as she walked towards the door.

She really is one good-looking broad, Matt thought. He figured she was around twenty-one or twenty-two years old. He motioned to the bartender.

"One more, Matt?" the bartender asked him.

"Yep. My last one. By the way, do you know what Sandra Peary's status is?" he asked.

The bartender grinned. "If you're asking if she's married, the answer is no."

Matt smiled. "What else do you know about her?"

"As far as I know, she's unattached. No steady boyfriend, but she hangs around with Pat McNally a lot. I think they're just friends, though. I've heard rumors that for the right price you can hit it."

"What the hell do you mean – for the right price?" Matt asked.

"Forget I said that. It's just gossip."

"What? Tell me," Matt insisted.

"Well, there was a guy in here one night – not a local, by the way – and Sandra and her folks were here and he looked over at her and made a remark."

"Like what kind of remark?" Matt asked.

"Something like, 'that's one expensive piece of ass sitting over there'. I'm pretty sure he meant Sandra and not her mother."

"Did he say anything else?"

"Nope. That was about it?"

"And, from that, you determined that she was selling it?" Matt inquired.

"Well, ya. What else could he have meant?"

Matt laughed. "I doubt he meant that. It's kinda a leap, don't you think?"

The bartender frowned. "Maybe. But, for some reason – maybe, the way he said it – I think he meant she was selling it."

Matt finished his beer and laid a couple of bucks on the bar. "Well, I wouldn't mind hitting it, but I sure as hell wouldn't pay for a piece of ass. Especially, not from anyone in this town."

"What? The women in Columbus aren't good enough for you?"

"Hell, they're all good enough. It's just that the whole town would know about it before I was finished."

Chapter Five

Chief Austin didn't look up when Officer Drollstrom walked into the room. It was after nine a.m. and Drollstrom had been scheduled to be at work by eight.

"Morning, Chief," Drollstrom said.

Totally ignoring Drollstrom, Austin picked up the phone and dialed 477, the number for the Farmer's and Merchant's Bank. He took a sip of his coffee, waiting for someone to answer his call. After ten rings and no answer, he hung up, wondering what was going on. The bank was supposed to open at nine a.m. City Hall, which housed the Police Department, was kiddy corner across the street from the bank, so he decided to walk over and check it out.

He emptied his coffee cup and stood up. "Be back in a few," he muttered to Drollstrom and walked out the door.

"Wait," Drollstrom yelled at him.

Austin stopped in the hallway for a split second, then, continued on his way.

Just as he was leaving the building, he saw Deputy Gorski get out of her squad car. She waved. "Where you off to?" she inquired, as she approached him.

"I need to talk to John Hobson at the bank," he told her.

"Is this about Debbie?"

"Her parents told me she had an account there. I need to check it out."

"What's the big deal?" Jacquie asked him.

24

"When her mom was going through some of her things, she found a bankbook for a savings account at F&M. She didn't know Debbie had an account there, and it seems there is a sizable balance. I want to verify the information."

"How sizable?"

"Over $7,000.00," Austin told her.

"No friggin' way," Jacquie exclaimed. "You gotta be kidding me. There's no way she could have saved that much from waitressing."

"My exact thoughts. I need to take a look at some bank statements. Maybe, they'll give us an idea of where the deposits came from and what she was up to."

"Let me know what you find," Jacquie told him, as she headed up the steps leading into City Hall.

"Will do," Austin said, as he started to cross the street.

"Chief?" Jacquie yelled.

Austin turned and looked at her. "What?"

"Is Pete in yet?"

Austin shook his head yes"

"Shit," Jacquie mumbled to herself, as she opened the door and entered the building.

John Hobson, President of Farmer's and Merchant's Bank, was sitting behind his desk looking at a copy of Debbie Nelson's savings account statement.

"Are you positive?" Chief Austin asked him.

"Absolutely. She made weekly deposits and they were all in cash. It's been going on for close to a year."

"Is it possible that a waitress could pull in that much money working for tips? It just seems excessive to me."

"I'd say it depends on the restaurant. If she worked for a pricey one, I guess it's possible, Augie."

"Do you know what restaurant she worked at?" Chief Austin asked the bank president.

"No idea. Don't her folks know?"

"They thought they did, but when John Nelson called the restaurant to inform the manager that she wouldn't be coming back to work, he had no idea who she was."

"Maybe, they got the name of the place wrong," Hobson commented.

"Or, maybe she didn't work as a waitress at all."

"You know, Augie, cocktail waitresses do pretty well. Perhaps, she was doing that kind of waitressing."

Austin sat back in the chair and thought about what Hobson had just said. "That makes sense, especially if she didn't want her folks to know. The cash deposits every week could have been tip money. Although, she probably would have been paid by check for her hourly wages. Do you recall her cashing checks here?"

"I wouldn't deal with that. I'll ask the tellers, but I don't think so. A lot of businesses will cash their employees' checks for them. Especially in low-paying jobs, like waitressing."

"Well, I guess I've got some digging to do," Chief Austin told Hobson. "Thanks for your time, John."

"Let me know if there's anything else I can do for you. Terrible business, this killing. She was a sweet girl, always smiling and friendly. Do you have any idea who could have done this?"

"Not a clue. But it's only been a day. I'm sure something will surface."

Deputy Gorski was on the phone when Chief Austin walked into the police station. He glanced over at Drollstrom's desk and frowned. Drollstrom had his feet on his desk, head resting against the wall, mouth open, and he was asleep. Austin walked over to him and pushed his feet off his desk, causing them to hit the floor hard.

"What the fuck?" Drollstrom yelled as he woke with a start. "What the hell do you. . ." He shut up when he realized that Austin was standing next to him.

"I have a job for you," Austin said, as he walked over to his desk and sat down.

Drollstrom glanced over at him. "What now?" he asked, his face red, embarrassed at being caught sleeping by his boss.

"I want you to go find your father and ask him if there is another job he could find for you. Tell him that this police business isn't for you and you need to do something else."

Officer Pete Drollstrom stared at him. "Are you nuts or something?" he said, laughing sarcastically. "I love this job."

"Do you really?" Austin asked.

"Of course. Where else could I get paid for driving around in a car and harassing people all day? Yes, sir, Chief. I love it and there's no way I'm quitting."

"Then, how about you start doing your job? I'm sick of your crap and your attitude, Pete. This bullshit has got to stop or, so help me God, I'll find a way to get rid of you."

"Dream on. My father's the mayor and as long as he's the mayor, there's no way you're gonna get rid of me."

"Don't be so sure. His term runs out next year and the talk is that he isn't going to get re-elected. So, maybe he should find you something else to do while he still has some clout in this town."

"He'll be elected again. He's always elected," Drollstrom said, bragging.

"Well, the way I see it is that if he's out, so are you."

Drollstrom grabbed his hat and headed for the door.

"Where do you think you're going?" Austin asked him.

"I'm going to get some breakfast at Earl's and then I'm gonna go see my father. I think he'll be very interested in hearing about this conversation."

"I'm sure he will. Don't let the door hit. . ." Austin watched as Drollstrom stormed out of the room. "Oh, to hell with it," he muttered.

Chapter Six

"There's no doubt?" Austin asked Dr. Severson, who was giving him the results of his preliminary findings.

"No doubt, Augie. She was asphyxiated. You know, smothered."

"I know what it means, Jerry. So, she was dead before she was thrown under the popcorn wagon," he stated.

"Looks like it. And, it looks like she was smothered with a pillow. I found a piece of a feather in her mouth."

"Which means that she probably was in a bed at the time," Austin said.

"Well, considering the fact that she had sex before she died, she probably was in a bed."

"This is gonna kill her parents. I was hoping it was a random killing, but this changes that. Obviously, she knew her killer."

"Probably," Severson agreed.

"What else do you have for me? Are the blood test results back yet?" Austin asked.

"Not all of them. She had been drinking, but she wasn't drunk. I'd say probably one or two drinks before she died. Her stomach contents showed she hadn't eaten for at least six hours. The welts on her back were from some type of whip, so she was probably into S&M. There were bruises on her wrists, probably from handcuffs. Again, probably used during S&M. Most of the bruising on her body was done before she died. The cuts and other injuries she sustained, when she was thrown out of a car, were post mortem."

"So, you figure she was thrown and not placed under the wagon on purpose?"

"The bruising is indicative of being thrown and the body rolling. I'd say she was thrown."

"When will you get the rest of the test results?" Austin inquired.

"A day or two. Augie, she was a young woman who had an extremely active sex life. And, I mean, super active."

"You don't think she was raped?" Austin asked.

"No, I don't. She did have some bruising in the vaginal area, but it wasn't recent. The bruising was already turning green, which indicates it happened at least six to seven days before her death."

"When you say super active sex life, just what are you referring to?"

Severson laughed. "I need to explain it to you? I mean she was getting laid on a regular basis and a lot. Once a night wasn't enough for whoever she was seeing."

Austin didn't say anything.

"You still there?" Severson asked.

"Sorry. Just thinking."

"Anything else?" the medical examiner asked Austin.

"Not for now. Call me when you have something more."

"I'll do that. Bye."

"Wait!" Austin yelled. "Don't hang up yet. I want to. . .." He stopped speaking when he realized he was talking to a dead phone.

Austin hung up the phone and sat back in his chair, thinking about what he had wanted to ask Severson. It's possible, he thought. And, it would sure explain a few things.

He looked up as Deputy Gorski walked into the room.

"Have you been by 4 corners this morning?" she asked him.

"No. Why?"

"The whole sidewalk alongside the popcorn wagon is covered with flowers, cards, and stuffed animals. It looks like some type of memorial to Debbie."

"People have to have a way to express their feelings, I guess," Austin said. "Debbie was well-liked in this town. I figure we're gonna see all kinds of emotions before we figure this out."

"Well, I know it pisses me off," Jacquie exclaimed.

"Jacquie?" Austin said, tentatively, dragging out her name.

"Yes."

"Have you ever heard of a house of ill repute around here?"

Jacquie looked at him, surprise written all over her face. Then, she laughed. "A whore house in Columbus? I don't think so. That is one secret that couldn't be kept in this town. In fact, I don't think any secret has ever been kept in this town."

Austin smiled. "Well, you're wrong there. But I can't go into that, can I? Then, I'd be telling you secrets."

"Funny. Anyway, what made you ask that question? You hear something?"

"Not exactly," he replied. "By the way," he said, changing the subject, "do you know who Debbie's boyfriend was?"

Jacquie thought for a second, then, frowned. "I don't know. I don't think she had one. At least, none that I know about."

"That's what her parents said, too."

"Why? What does that have to do with this?"

"Maybe nothing. But it seems to me that for someone who didn't have a boyfriend, she sure was having a lot of sex."

Jacquie stared at him. Suddenly, it dawned on her what he was getting at. "No way, Chief. Not in this town."

"And, why not?" he asked. "What makes this town so different from hundreds of others?"

Jacquie started to say something, then, stopped.

"Well?" Austin asked again.

"Because. . ."

"Because what?"

"Because it's Columbus, that's why," she blurted out.

Chapter Seven

Chief Austin and Deputy Gorski spent the rest of the day interviewing Debbie Nelson's family and friends. Mary Nelson, Debbie's oldest sister, told Austin that she hadn't seen Debbie in a few weeks, but if there had been a man in her life, she would have known about it. "Debbie tells me everything," she told Austin.

He smiled sympathetically, told the family again how sorry he was for their loss, and left the Nelson home. Mary had given him the names of Debbie's best friends and he decided to drive over to their apartment and talk to them. He figured it would probably be a wasted trip, as he doubted anyone would be home in the middle of a Monday afternoon.

Therefore, he was surprised when the door was opened by a pretty young woman, who was holding a drink in her hand.

"Chief Austin," she said. "Come on in. It's about Debbie, isn't it?"

He looked her over as he entered the apartment and followed her into the living room. Two more attractive women were sitting on the couch, each holding a cocktail.

"Can I fix you something to drink?" Annie asked.

He smiled. "No thanks. I'm on duty."

"Of course. How silly of me," she said. "Please sit down."

"Annie, isn't it?" He inquired. "Annie Berg?"

"You got it right. You remember Karen Berke and Rose Thomas, don't you?" she asked him.

"Of course. Nice to see you all."

"We're devastated over what happened to Debbie," Rose replied. "She was a wonderful. . ." She broke up and started sobbing.

"I'm truly sorry to bother you," Austin said. "I need to ask you a few questions about Debbie. I'll be as brief as possible."

"Anything we can do to help. Please, ask away," Annie told him.

Austin looked over at Rose who was reaching for a tissue. "Are you okay, Rose?" he asked her.

"I'm fine. I just can't believe she's dead. She was my best friend, you know. Can't we do this some other time?" she asked him.

"I'm very sorry. I know this is hard, but it's best if I talk to you now."

"Of course," Rose said.

"I need to know who Debbie was seeing. There's no doubt that she was involved with someone. Her parents don't know who it was. I'm hoping one of you can help me out. I guess that would be you, Rose."

Rose looked at him, confused. "Why me? Why would she tell me?"

"Well, you just told me she was your best friend. I figure she would have told her best friend what was going on in her love life."

Rose let out a sigh of relief. "Oh, that," she said and blew her nose. "Sorry."

"Take your time." He waited for her to respond. "So, did she?" Austin finally asked her again.

"Did she what?" Rose responded.

"Did Debbie tell you who she was seeing?"

Austin asked, patiently.

Rose shrugged. "I have no idea. If she was seeing someone, it's news to me. How about you Annie? Karen? Did she tell you guys?"

"The last guy that she mentioned to me was Ronny Ott and they broke up months ago. Other than that, I haven't got a clue," Annie said. "What about you, Karen."

Karen took a sip of her drink. She thought for a few seconds and said, "Nope. Sorry. She never said anything to me either."

Austin looked at the three of them, wondering what the hell was going on.

"Don't you girls work?" he asked, changing the subject.

Rose giggled, obviously a little drunk. "Not today."

"That's a little strange, isn't it? All three of you are off on Mondays. How'd you work that out?"

"I don't know," Rose said. She looked over at Annie. "How'd we work that out, Annie?" she asked, giggling.

"I'm sorry, Chief Austin. We've been drinking and it looks like Rose has about had it. I think it's time we put her to bed," Annie remarked. "We thought having a drink and toasting Debbie was a good idea. We should have stopped at one, I guess."

Austin said. "Just a couple more questions and I'll be out of your hair."

"Of course," Annie replied.

"What are your jobs?" he asked.

"Well, Rose and I work at Shelby's in Sun Prairie

and Karen is between jobs right now. Sandra is a. . ." She quit talking, hoping that Austin didn't catch her slip.

"Is that Shelby's Nightclub?"

"That's right. They're closed on Mondays, so we're not working today."

"So, you're cocktail waitresses?" Austin asked her.

"That's right," Annie told him.

"Is there good money in that?" he inquired.

"It pays the rent," Annie answered, smiling.

"Do you know where Debbie worked?" he asked.

"She worked at. . ." Annie stopped and turned to Karen. "What was the name of the place?" she asked.

Karen got a blank look on her face, and she shook her head. "I don't remember. How about you, Rose? Do you remember where Debbie worked?"

Rose slowly opened her eyes and looked over at Karen. "Did you say something?"

Annie smiled at Austin. "Sorry. I guess we're all drawing a blank."

"I see. Well, I guess that's about it." He stood and started to walk towards the door to leave. "One more thing," he said. "You girls have lived in this town all your lives. Have you ever heard anything about a whore house in the area?"

They were silent. He waited for one of them to answer, guessing it would be Annie.

Annie it was. "You have got to be kidding," she answered after a few seconds, looking amused. "Around here? In Columbus? I don't think so."

"Well, it doesn't have to be in Columbus. It could

be out towards Beaver Dam or Sun Prairie. Even Fall River. It's just something I heard. Gossip, you know."

"Sorry, Chief. I can't help you," Annie said. She looked at Karen and Rose. "How about you guys? Have you ever heard of a whorehouse around here?"

Karen grinned and shook her head no.

"Is there anything else?" Annie asked.

"That's it for now. Thanks for your time, ladies. Please, let me know if you think of anything that might seem important. Sometimes, even the smallest thing can help."

The three women called out their goodbyes, as Austin opened the door to leave.

"Oh, one more thing," he said. "Is that Sandra Peary you were talking about?"

He waited for an answer.

Finally, Annie said, "It was."

"Do you think that she's home right now?"

"Probably," Annie said.

"Could you give me her address?" Austin asked her. "I should probably go talk to her."

"I doubt she'll be able to tell you anything more than we were," Annie informed him.

"That might be, but I still need to talk to her."

"She rents the apartment above Rosalee Vollier's shop."

"Really. I didn't know Rosalee had rented it out," Austin commented.

"Well, she has," Annie declared. "Is there anything else, Chief?"

Austin walked through the door, then turned back and looked at the three women. 'There is one

37

more thing you could help me with," he said. "Do any of you have an idea how Debbie was able to save over $7,000.00 in less than a year?"

Chapter Eight

Chief Austin opened the outside door, looked inside, and sighed. There were a lot of stairs to climb and his hip had been hurting for the past few days. He started walking up the steps, then, stopped and waited when he heard a door slam shut above him. Sandra Peary came tearing down the steps, obviously in a hurry. She stopped when she realized that Austin was standing on the stairs below her.

"Hi," she said, smiling. "Are you lost?"

Austin smiled back at her. "I sure hope not," he answered. "Actually, you just saved me a trip up these stairs." He looked up at the top landing. "How many are there?"

Sandra laughed. "A lot. I've never counted them. I gather you want to talk to me."

"I do, and here you are. Perhaps, we could just sit on the bottom step and talk for a few minutes."

Sandra frowned. "I really need to go. I'm already late for a hair appointment. What's this about?"

"I need to ask you a few questions about Debbie," Austin told her.

"It's horrible, isn't it? I'd love to talk, but could we possibly do this later? I could come over to the station in an hour or so if that would be okay. Pretty please." She smiled seductively and he realized that she probably got anything she wanted when she turned on the charm.

Before he realized it, the words were out of his mouth. "That's fine. Any time is fine."

Sandra stood up and ran out the door. "Thanks.

I'll see you later."

Austin watched as the door closed, wondering what the hell had just happened.

"Where's Drollstrom?" Chief Austin yelled as he stood in the doorway of the police station.

Deputy Gorski looked up from her desk, surprised. Austin rarely raised his voice, much less yelled. "He's in the bathroom," she told him.

Austin looked at the coffee pot sitting on a table in the back of the room. "Isn't there any coffee?" he asked.

"No. I just cleaned the pot, but I'll make some if you want."

"Forget it. No, wait. Make a pot, will you? I'm gonna be here for a while and I need a pick me up."

"What's got you so upset?" Jacquie asked.

"Have you seen Drollstrom's squad car?"

"No. I haven't been out of the building since two. What's the problem with the car?" Jacquie inquired.

"The back end is all caved in. It looks like he backed into something. I swear I don't know what. . ." He quit talking as the door opened and Drollstrom walked in.

"Man, did I bomb that bowl. I thought I was gonna shit my pants for a second," he said, looking at Jacquie.

"Too much information," Jacquie said, disgustedly.

"Way too much. Watch your mouth, Pete."

Drollstrom looked surprised seeing Austin there. "When did you get back?" he asked defensively.

40

"Never mind about me. What happened to the squad car?" Austin asked him.

"What about it?"

"What did you back into?"

Drollstrom glared at him. "What makes you think it was my fault? Maybe, somebody hit me. Did you ever think about that?"

Austin shook his head no. "If you're around when something bad happens, I can be sure it's your fault. So, what happened?"

"I don't know what you're so upset about. It's just a car. It can be fixed."

Austin stared at him, trying to control his temper. "It's an expensive car and it's police property, Pete. What happened?"

Drollstrom walked over to his desk and sat down. "Damndest thing. I pulled into Hewitt's gas station to turn around. I've done it a million times and never had a problem. I guess this car must have pulled in after me and when I put my car in reverse, I hit him. Basically, it was his fault. He shouldn't have been following so close. Anyway, I never saw him behind me."

Austin stared at him, trying to keep his cool. "So, you backed into a car. How much damage to his vehicle?"

"Well, it wasn't really a car. It was a truck. A big-ass pickup truck. His bumper had some damage, but not that bad. Don't worry, though. I ticketed him for following too close. His insurance should cover it."

Austin glared at him. "So, you backed into him and then you gave him a ticket? And, just how do you figure his insurance is going to cover the damage when it's your fault?" he quietly asked.

Drollstrom didn't say anything.

"Well, Pete?"

"It's his word against mine. I'm a cop. Who do you think the judge will believe?"

"Let me see a copy of the ticket," Austin said.

"Why?"

"Just give it to me," Austin yelled.

"It's in the car."

"Then, go get it," Austin told him.

Drollstrom stood up and walked out of the room, slamming the door behind him.

"What are you going to do?" Jacquie asked him.

"I'm going to make Pete call the driver of the truck and apologize, tell him to tear up the ticket, and to submit any claims for damage done to his vehicle. And, I'm going to inform Drollstrom that he is going to pay for the repair to the squad car."

"He won't pay, you know," Jacquie said.

"Oh, he's gonna pay all right. I'll take it out of his paychecks."

"The mayor will probably put up a fuss," Jacquie told him.

"Let him. I'm sick of that entire family."

Drollstrom walked back into the station and threw his ticket pad down on Austin's desk.

"Here," he muttered.

"Go sit down," Austin told him.

Austin watched as Drollstrom threw himself into his chair, causing it to roll back and hit the wall.

"You damage that wall, you're gonna pay for

that, too," Austin told Drollstrom.

"Whataya mean, too?"

"You're paying the repair bill for the squad car," he informed Drollstrom.

"Like hell, I am."

Austin flipped through the copies of tickets that were in the front of the pad. He found the one he was looking for and tore it out. He held it out to Drollstrom, and said, "Here. Call this guy and tell him to forget about the ticket."

Drollstrom stared at him like he was a foreign object. "No way," he said, sneering. "I'm not calling him."

Chief Austin got up and walked behind Drollstrom, pulled a length of rope out of his pocket, put it around Drollstrom's neck, and pulled. Drollstrom reached for the rope and struggled to pull it free from his neck. Austin pulled harder, twisting the rope until Drollstrom's hands fell to his sides. Austin watched as Drollstrom's tongue bulged out of his mouth, enlarged and blue. Finally, after a minute or so, Drollstrom made a gurgling sound and his entire body went limp. Austin glanced over at Jacquie and declared, "That was more work than I thought it would be."

"I'm sorry," Jacquie said, looking confused. "What was more work?"

Austin stared at her, his face starting to turn red. "Did I say that out loud?" he asked.

"You did," Jacquie replied.

"Forget it," he told her. He turned to Drollstrom,

who was staring at him. "Get out of here," he said softly.

"I've still got an hour left on my shift," Drollstrom said.

Jacquie, concerned about the strange look on Austin's face, said, "Pete, I think you better leave. Now!"

Drollstrom stood up and walked out of the room. "Fuck you both," he yelled, as he slammed the door shut.

Chapter Nine

Chief Augie Austin looked up at the clock on the wall. "Shit," he muttered.

Officer Benisch glanced up from his desk. "What's the matter?" he asked.

"Look at the time," Austin said. "It's seven-thirty already. Why didn't you say something?"

Benisch looked confused. "I didn't know I was supposed to. What's the problem?"

"We have a church thing tonight. Catherine is going to kill me for being late again."

"So, go now. What's the difference if you're a little late?"

"Have you met my wife?" Austin asked, jokingly.

Benisch laughed. "I see what you mean. You better get out of here."

The phone rang as Austin stood up to leave. He glanced over at Benisch and waited to see what the call was about. His heart sunk as he watched the expression on his officer's face turn grim.

"We'll be right there," Benisch said. He listened to the caller for a few more seconds and said, "Got it."

"What is it?" Austin asked him, as soon as Benisch hung up the phone.

"Bob Hein just pulled a body out of the Crawfish River."

"Where at?" Austin asked.

"He said to meet him at the back of the canning factory. I'm not sure where he found the body. Do you want me to call Doc Severson?"

"I'll call him. You head on over there and make

45

sure no one disturbs anything. I'll be right behind you. I need to call home and let the kids know I'm gonna be late."

"Will do," Benisch said, as he grabbed the keys for the squad car and headed towards the door.

"Benny, wait," Austin said.

Benisch stopped and looked at him. "What?"

"We'll want some pictures. Call the Journal before you go and see if Kirk Peary is available."

"He's most likely at home having dinner. The paper is closed for the day," Benisch said, as he reached for the phone on his desk.

"Never mind. You get on over to the canning factory. I'll call him."

"Okay. I'll see you there," Benisch said and started out the door.

"Benny?" Austin called.

Benny turned and looked at him. "What?"

"Did Bob say if it's one of the Mexicans?"

"No. It's not. It's. . ."

"I knew it. It's a Jamaican, isn't it? It was only a matter of time before they started killing each other. They're constantly fighting about one thing or the other," Austin interrupted.

"Sorry, Chief. Bob said that it's a woman."

"Shit!" Austin exclaimed. "Not another one."

"It looks like it." Benisch hesitated, then, he ran out of the office before Austin could ask him anything else.

Bob Hein, the manager of Stokely-Van Camp Canning Factory, was waiting when Benisch pulled up and parked. Benisch jumped out of his car and walked over to Hein. "Where is she?" he asked.

Bob motioned for Benisch to follow him and led him toward the back of the building. "It isn't pretty," he told Benisch. "Is Chief Austin on his way?"

"He is. He was going to call the medical examiner before he left the station. You didn't touch anything, did you?"

"Well, of course, I did. I pulled her out of the water. I couldn't just leave her there to float away. But that's all I did."

"Do you know who it is?" Benisch asked as they walked towards the river.

"Nah., I don't recall ever seeing her before. It isn't one of ours."

"You know all your employees?"

"Every one of them. I make it a point to know them and that includes the Mexicans and Jamaicans."

"Austin figured it was one of them that you found. We get a lot of disturbance calls while they're in town," Benisch told him.

"Well, they live in close quarters and those huts get pretty hot. It doesn't take much to set them off." Hein pointed to a spot alongside the river. "There she is," he said.

Benisch walked over to a body lying on the grass. The woman was clad in only a bra and panties and his first thought was to cover her. He bent down to get a better look at the woman's face and felt ill. It was a local girl. Even soaking wet, there was no mistaking that flaming red hair.

"It's Arlis Upton," he told Hein. "She grew up in

47

a house just down the street from here."

"I know that family." He looked down at the body and then looked away. "I can't believe I didn't recognize her. What do you think happened?" Hein asked.

"Damned if I know. We'll have to wait for the medical examiner to determine that. Although, there are marks on her neck. I'd say she was probably strangled."

"Horrible way to go," Hein said. "Do you think she was strangled and then thrown into the Crawfish?"

"It could have happened that way," Benisch declared. "Or, she might have been alive when she entered the water and drowned. Whatever. It doesn't pay to speculate." He turned as he heard a siren. "Looks like Augie's here," he told Hein.

Dr. Severson arrived thirty minutes after Chief Austin. He took one look at the body and declared that the woman was dead.

Austin looked at him, questioningly. "You think?" he said, sarcastically. "It's a little obvious, Jerry."

Severson glanced up at him, from where he was kneeling on the grass, and grinned. "New rule. All coroners and medical examiners have to declare that the body is dead before they continue any examination."

"Isn't that all that coroners do anyway?" Benisch asked him.

"Most of them. Some are actual doctors. Anyway, this woman is dead."

"She has marks on her neck," Austin said.

"Maybe she drowned or maybe she was strangled," Severson replied. "I'll know more when I get her on the table." He stood up and shook his head. "Damn shame. She was a beautiful woman. What's going on in Columbus, Austin? Two women found dead in two days."

Chief Austin didn't answer him.

Severson looked at him. "You okay?" he asked Austin.

"No," Austin replied. "I'm not okay, and I don't think I'll be okay until 1 find the sick son of a bitch that did this."

"Can you cover her up?" Hein asked. "It doesn't seem right to be staring at her like this."

"We need to take pictures of the body first. Kirk pulled in behind me," Austin informed him.

"He's taking his own sweet time getting over here," Hein commented.

"He said he had to load his camera with fresh film," Austin stared down at the body and sighed. "I'm gonna go get a blanket out of my car," he said, and walked back towards his squad car, passing Kirk Peary on his way.

"He looks pretty upset," Peary remarked as he approached the men.

"Of course, he's upset," Benisch exclaimed. "We're all upset. He's got a teenage daughter not much younger than these young women, and we don't have a clue as to what's going on."

Chapter Ten

At six a.m. the next morning, Dr. Severson and Chief Austin were sitting in a booth at Earl's Cafe. Severson took a sip of coffee, made a face, and added a teaspoon of sugar.

"Like it sweet, do ya?" Austin said.

"I do. Just like my women."

"What did you find?"

"The Nelson woman was probably drunk when she was killed," he told Chief Austin. "She also had drugs in her system."

"You got the toxicology report pretty fast," Austin commented.

"We're still checking for other things, but drugs are easy to spot in a blood test. By the way, I believe the last thing she ate was spaghetti, but that's not written in stone."

"Why not?" Austin asked.

"Most of her stomach contents had already been digested. However, it was definitely some type of Italian food. She probably ate around six o'clock or so Saturday night."

"What about Arlis Upton? Did you find alcohol and drugs in her, too?"

"Not with the initial tests we've run. I'll know more in a day or two.

"What about the time of death?"

"I put Debbie Nelson's death between twelve and two Sunday morning. Arlis Upton's time of death was a little harder to determine, seeing as how she was in the water. But, taking the temperature of the water into consideration, I would guess that she was most likely murdered around the same time."

"So, your final determination is that Arlis was murdered."

"She was definitely murdered. Asphyxiated.

"She was strangled?"

"Yes. Her hyoid bone was broken. Actually, it was crushed. Whoever killed her was strong. She put up a fight, though. I don't think she went easy," Severson told him.

"You're saying she was killed around the same time as Debbie. But that doesn't make any sense, Jerry. Why dispose of Debbie in the middle of downtown, where anyone driving by could find her but dump Arlis' body in the river? Why not dump them in the same location?"

Severson took a sip of coffee. "Beats me. Of course, you're assuming it was the same person who killed both of them. I just find out the how. It's up to you to figure out the who and the why."

Georgie walked over to the men's booth, holding a fresh pot of coffee. "You two need a fill-up?" she asked.

Austin smiled up at her. "I'm good. How about you?" he asked Severson.

"Just half a cup, please. I've got to back to work."

Georgie poured the coffee, then, laid the check on the table. "Whenever you're ready," she stated and walked back behind the counter.

Severson took a swallow of coffee. "Good coffee," he remarked.

"Best in town," Austin said. "What else did you find?"

"It's all in the prelim reports I just gave you. You'll have the final ones by the end of the week or Monday at the latest. It might be a coincidence that they were murdered around the same time, Jerry."

"Was Arlis sexually assaulted?"

"I don't think so. There's no doubt that Debbie had sex before she was killed. It was harder to determine that fact with Arlis, her being in the water and all. She was sexually active but not to the degree that Nelson was. I don't think either woman was raped before she was killed."

Chief Austin lit up a cigarette, sat back, and gave Severson a questioning look.

"What?" Severson asked.

"Jerry, have you ever heard about a cat house in or around Columbus?"

Severson laughed. "You're kidding, right?"

"Not at all. Debbie showed signs of having had rough sex, which possibly included S&M. From what you've told me, she was extremely sexually active. She also had a sizable savings account and no one can explain where the money came from. I haven't found any accounts for Arlis yet but that doesn't mean there aren't any. And, there are several young women in town who I think are involved in what happened. Or, at least they know something about it and aren't talking. Everything about these murders yells sex."

Severson studied Austin's face, not sure if he was serious. "Isn't everything?" he said, after a few seconds.

"Isn't everything what?"

"About sex. Isn't everything about sex? And, money, of course. Let's not forget about the money."

"I thought I knew everything that goes on in this town. Now, I'm not so sure," Austin said. "I'm probably grasping at straws about the whore house thing. It's just that all the signs are there."

"If there is a house of ill repute," Severson said, "it doesn't necessarily have to be in Columbus. These girls – if they were prostituting themselves – could have worked any place – any town. I'd say it's possible with the Nelson woman, but I doubt that Upton was involved in prostitution."

"Why one and not the other?" Austin asked.

"Debbie had all the signs of leading a rough life. Arlis' examination, on the other hand, was what I would expect to find in a healthy young woman. I don't believe she was into anything kinky."

Austin frowned. "So, you think we're looking for two killers, which would explain why they were found in two locations. That makes more sense. If the same person murdered both of them, why dump one woman downtown and the other one in the river? Shit! You've just made my life more complicated," Austin said, raising his voice. He glanced around the café to see if any of the other customers were watching him. "Sorry," he told Severson. "I didn't mean to get so vocal."

"I understand your frustration," Severson replied. "I wish I could help you out, but I'm as much in the dark as you are. I figure, though, that there's someone in every town that knows every time someone takes a dump. You got somebody like that living here that you can talk to?"

"Fuck!" Austin uttered.

"What?"

"Drollstrom. That asshole knows everything that goes on here and he's the last person I'd ask for help."

"He is kind of a jerk, isn't he?" Severson said, grinning.

"It's not funny, Jerry. The only reason he's even on the force is because his father is the fucking mayor. He bugs the hell out of me."

"So, get rid of him. What's the difference if his father is a big shot in this town?"

"I can't. If he goes, I go."

Severson stared at Austin, confused at what he had just heard. "Explain that, please," he said.

Austin sighed. "After Chief Caldwell stepped down in the middle of his term, I was appointed to take his place. The only way Mayor Drollstrom would agree to this was if I gave his idiot son a job. I signed an agreement saying that, as long as I was Police Chief, I would keep Pete on the force."

"I'm confused here, Augie. You're voted in by the people here in town every time there's an election. Why do you have to keep him?"

"When the Mayor added that clause, saying that I would give his son a job, the wording was deceiving. The short version of this story is that I agreed to keep Pete on the force until he decided to quit. What I misunderstood was that I agreed not to fire Pete as long as I was on the job. I thought it meant until the appointment was over and an election was held, so I signed it. I figured I could put up with him until that happened. Obviously, I screwed up. So, I'm stuck with him."

"That doesn't seem right to me. Have you had an attorney look at that agreement?"

"Oh, yes. Years ago, right after the first time I was elected and tried to fire him. According to Cuddehey, the attorney I talked to, I didn't have a leg to stand on. And, since that day, Pete throws it in my face every chance he gets."

"Did you ever consider that Cuddehey might be in the mayor's pocket?"

Austin shook his head. "Not really. Do you think that's a possibility?"

"Anything is possible, my friend. But, if I were you, I'd certainly go see a different attorney. Perhaps, someone who doesn't live in this town."

"I just might do that," Austin said. "I guess a second opinion never hurts. With my luck, though, he'll probably say the agreement is binding."

"Then, your hands will be tied forever," Severson declared.

"It looks that way. Unless the kid quits, which will never happen," Austin said, as he lit another cigarette.

"Or, dies," Severson added.

Chapter Eleven

The Crawfish River runs through Columbus. It enters the northeast part of town just south of Lewis Street, flows through an area of the town called Little Mexico, drifts along under a bridge on Ludington Street, and passes the back side of the canning factory. It continues moving south to River Road and snakes its way out of town. Normally, it is slow-moving and, in some areas, so narrow you can jump across it.

Chief Austin parked his car on the side of the road and walked over to the small bridge. The water level was about average for that time of year, especially since the area had not had any violent thunderstorms yet this summer.

He walked over to the other side of the road and stared at the water as it flowed toward the back of the canning factory. He wondered where Arlis' body had been dumped for it to wind up stuck on a log in the middle of the river. He was pretty sure that she had been dumped north of where he was now standing.

Austin took one last look at the water and walked back to his squad car. Time to do a land search, he thought as he pulled a uey and drove away.

Deputy Gorski and Officer Drollstrom were both sitting at their desks when Chief Austin walked into the police station. He glanced over at Drollstrom, who was drinking from a large container that came from the A & W Drive-In.

"What's in the cup? Root beer?"

Drollstrom gave him a strange look. "Ya. Why?"

he said, suspiciously.

"Just wondering." Austin walked over to his desk and sat down. He checked his messages, sorting out what he thought was important from the nuisance calls. He glanced over at Drollstrom, who was taking a sip of his root beer. "I have a job for you, Pete."

Drollstrom stared at his boss, not sure if he heard correctly. "Did you just say you have something for me to do?"

"If you don't mind."

"What is it?" he asked, wondering why Austin was being so nice.

"I want you to head up a search party. I want you to call Benny, Matt, and Sam and see if they are available to work some extra hours. I figure the four of you should be able to handle the job."

Drollstrom's face lit up. "Sure thing," he said, surprised at the request. "What are we searching for?"

"Do you know the spot where Arlis Upton's body was found?"

"Of course, I do. Good fishing. I throw a line in there every so often. So, what about it?"

"I want you to start there and search the area. Work north towards Lewis Street. I guess two guys on each side of the river will have to do unless you've got some friends who might want to help."

Officer Drollstrom stared at him; confusion written all over his face. "Why?" he finally asked.

"We need to find out where Arlis Upton went into the water. I want you to go through every inch of grass and every bush until you get to Lewis Street. You can stop after you pass the last house on the street, just past the cemetery."

Drollstrom nodded his head. "Right. We're looking for evidence."

"That's right, Pete. Don't leave a stone unturned."

"All the stones or just the big ones?" Drollstrom asked, joking.

Austin forced himself to grin at the lame remark. "Just do the best you can. Hopefully, you'll find something that will tell us where Arlis was thrown in."

Drollstrom grabbed his hat off his desk and started to leave the room.

Deputy Gorski looked over at her boss. Austin shook his head, obviously annoyed. "Pete," she called.

He turned around and looked at her. "What?" he asked.

"I think you're supposed to call Benny, Matt, and Sam before you leave."

Drollstrom grinned. "Right. I guess I better do that first. And, I think I'll call mom and ask her to make us some snacks. We may get hungry out there."

"You do understand that you're not going on a picnic, don't you?" Austin asked.

"I know," Pete said.

"Just be sure you take water. It's gonna be a hot one today." He got up from his desk and walked towards the door "You good, then?" he asked Drollstrom.

"I'm good," Drollstrom replied.

"I'll see you later," Austin told Jacquie.

"Where are you going?" Jacquie asked.

"Sandra Peary never came in yesterday, did

she?"

"Not while I was here," Jacquie said.

"Well, it's time her and I had a talk."

Jacquie grinned. "Do you think you're up to climbing all those stairs? What if she isn't there? You would have made the trip for nothing."

Austin thought for a few seconds and walked back to his desk. "You got a phone number for her?" he asked Jacquie.

Jacquie grinned, picked up the telephone directory, and looked up Sandra's phone number. "933," she told him.

Austin dialed the number and waited. "No answer," he finally said and hung up.

"It's a good thing you called," Jacquie said, smugly. "Now, I don't have to worry about finding you lying at the bottom of the stairs.

"Very funny. You know, I'm not so damned old that I can't climb a flight of stairs. I just have a bad hip."

"I remember. Old football injury. Right?"

"That's right. And, don't forget it," Austin exclaimed, as he left the room, slamming the door behind him.

"Touchy subject," Pete commented.

"Sure is," Jacquie replied. "They lost that game."

Chapter Twelve

"You're a hard one to pin down," Austin told Sandra.

"Sorry. The last couple of days have been really busy."

"You were supposed to come in and talk to me yesterday."

"As I said, I've been busy," she replied.

"What can you tell me about Debbie Nelson?"

"What do you want to know?"

Austin sat back and looked her in the eyes. "I want to know what she was up to. I want to know why she was killed. I want to know why she was thrown out of a car onto the street like a bag of garbage. I want to know if there's a prostitution ring here in my town and I want to know if you're part of it."

"What?" she asked, looking totally shocked at his last sentence. "You think I'm a prostitute? My god, Chief, you've known me most of my life. How can you ask me that?"

"I have to ask. Are you?"

"Of course not," she answered, tears welling up in her eyes. "My God, I can't believe you could think that of me." She started crying and reached for her purse.

"I'm sorry, Sandra. I had to ask." Austin got up and walked over to Jacquie's desk and grabbed a box of tissue. "Here," he said, handing her the box.

"Thank you," she said.

Austin watched as she dried her eyes and blew her nose, trying to decide if this was real or an act.

Sandra smiled at him and took a deep breath. "Sorry. I've been a ball of nerves ever since Debbie was killed. She was a good friend, you know."

"Are you okay to continue?" he asked her.

"I'm fine. And, the answer is no. I'm not a whore."

"I didn't think you were. But I had to ask. There's some talk around town of a whore house somewhere in the area and - well, the truth is - it looks like Debbie might have been part of it."

"No way," Sandra exclaimed. "There's no way she was part of anything that sick."

"Do you know if Debbie was in a relationship?"

"I don't think so."

"Well, with you being good friends and all, she would have told you if she was. Right?" Austin asked.

"Probably. At least, I think she would have. She was a pretty private person, though. I guess she could have been involved with someone and not told me."

"Who else would she have told? How about Annie or Karen or Rose? Would she have told one of them?"

Sandra thought for a second or two and then shook her head no. "I don't think they would know if I don't. But you should probably ask them."

"I did."

"And. . ."

"It seems they were kept in the dark, too. Maybe Debbie wasn't as good a friend as you all thought she was," Austin declared.

Sandra looked down, not responding to his comment.

61

"Did Annie or one of the others tell you that I had talked to them?"

"No. I haven't talked to them. Like I said, I've been busy."

"So, none of them called you and told you that I interviewed them and what we talked about? I find that unusual if you're such good friends."

"Chief Austin, we're friends. We're not joined at the hips. We get together once in a while and go out for dinner or a few drinks but we lead separate lives. It's not that unusual that we don't spend every waking minute talking to each other and telling each other every aspect of our lives," Sandra said, sounding defensive.

Austin shook his head in agreement. "I'm sorry. I forget that you're grown women. Now, on the other hand, my daughter, Leslie, is on the phone constantly, telling her friends everything that happens. I guess when you grow up that comes to an end."

Sandra smiled. "It doesn't end. It just slows down. I think we learn to filter what to talk about and what to keep private."

"What can you tell me about Debbie's old boyfriend, Ronny Ott?"

Sandra looked confused. "Ronny? She broke up with him ages ago. Why? Do you think he had something to do with Debbie's murder?"

"Just asking, is all. Do you know him?"

Sandra thought for a minute. "I do, but not very well. While Debbie was going out with him, they pretty much kept to themselves. We all figured they'd get married, but all of a sudden they broke up. She never really talked about it and we never knew why. As far as I know, he's a pretty nice guy. I never heard her complain or say anything bad about him."

"What about Arlis Upton? How well did you know her?"

"My God, isn't that horrible? Poor Arlis, drowning in the Crawfish River. It makes me sick just to think about it."

"Arlis didn't drown. She was strangled."

Sandra looked surprised. "She was murdered?"

"How well did you know her?" he asked again.

"Hardly at all. I knew her from school and all, but we never hung out together."

"When was the last time you saw her?" Austin asked.

Sandra puffed up her cheeks and blew the air out, thinking about the question. "I don't know," she said. "It's been a while."

"So, she never hung out with you and your friends?"

"Never," Sandra said, shaking her head no.

"Do you have any idea who her friends were?"

"Not really," Sandra answered. "She still lived at home. Why not ask her dad?"

"I did. He has no idea."

"I'm not surprised at that. He's out of town a lot and they didn't really get along. Why don't you ask her boyfriend?"

"She had a boyfriend? Do you know who it is??"

Sandra gave him a funny look, wondering if he was serious. "You don't know?" she asked after a few seconds.

Austin shook his head no. "I have no idea," he told her.

"It's Sam Lober."

Austin looked surprised. "My Sam Lober? That's who she was going with?"

"That's right. Your man, Sam."

Chapter Thirteen

Austin waited until Sandra Peary was out of the police station before he picked up the phone. He started to dial Sam Lober's number, remembered he was out with Drollstrom searching for clues and hung up. Austin was pissed. He had interviewed numerous people and no one had mentioned Sam. How could he not know that one of his officers had been involved with Arlis Upton?

He glanced up at the clock. It was already four and he wanted to talk to Ronny Ott. Although he was told that Debbie's and Ronny's breakup was amicable, he needed to find out the reason they split up. He checked some notes and headed out of the station.

Deputy Jacquie Gorski was coming up the stairs, a smile on her face. "Chief," she stated, acknowledging him. "Where are you off to?"

"Did you know that Sam Lober was dating Arlis Upton?" he yelled at her.

"Whoa. What are you yelling at me for?"

Austin took a deep breath and let the air out. "I'm yelling at you because you're supposed to let me know what's going on around here. I just found out that Arlis Upton was dating Sam. Why didn't you say something yesterday, when her body was found floating in that filthy river?"

Jacquie looked confused. "I'm sorry. I thought you knew. Sam's been dating Arlis for over six months now. It's common knowledge. No one was trying to keep it a secret."

"Well, I just heard about it. You know what this

means, don't you?"

"Shit!" Jacquie declared as she realized why he was so upset. "He's a suspect in her murder."

"He is until he's cleared," Austin declared.

"And, he's out looking for evidence with Drollstrom. You've got to pull him off this case," Jacquie told him.

"Of course, I do."

"You don't really think he had anything to do with her death, do you?"

"Of course not. But we've got to go by the book, Jacquie. We can't afford any screw-ups. Do you know how far they've gone with their search?"

"It's been a few hours since they started. God, Chief, I have no idea where they might be by now."

"I'm gonna drive around and see if I can spot them."

"Should I try to get Pete on the radio? He may be close enough to hear it?"

"You can try. If he answers, find out where he is and then let me know," Austin said and ran out of the building.

Austin was making a left turn, heading into Little Mexico when he got the call on his radio. It was Jacquie, telling him that the 'boys' were back and he should return to the station.

He made a u-turn and returned to the station.

Austin walked up the stairs into City Hall and headed around the corner into the police station. He stopped in the doorway and looked around the noisy room. Jacquie and Drollstrom were sitting at their desks, while Officers Benisch, Leyson, and Lober were standing by the small table that held the coffee pot. Everyone seemed to be talking at the same time and he realized that this was probably the first time, since the Christmas party, that all of his officers were together.

Jacquie glanced over at the door, saw her boss standing there, and yelled, "Quiet. The Chief is here."

The room went quiet as Austin walked over to his desk. "Is there any coffee left?" he asked.

"Sure is," Leyson said, as he poured a cup and handed it to Austin.

"Thanks," Austin said, as he took the coffee. "I guess you either finished searching or you found something and that's the reason you're all back here," he declared.

Drollstrom, no longer able to control himself, jumped out of his chair and handed Austin an evidence bag. "We found where she was thrown in," he stated confidently.

"Did you tape off the area?"

Drollstrom gave him a blank stare.

"You just said you found the place where Arlis Upton's body was dumped into the river. Did you tape off the area?" Austin asked again.

"Well, I think we . . ."

"As far as I can see, everyone's here. So, who is there keeping eyes on things to make sure nothing is disturbed?"

"Well, no one. There's no reason for anyone to be there. We went over the entire area and there's nothing else there," Drollstrom said. "Take a look at what we found."

Austin looked at the clear plastic bag that Drollstrom had handed him. He could see a woman's high heel shoe inside. He glanced over at Drollstrom. "Where did you find this?"

"On the shore behind the Nickerson house."

"In Little Mexico?" Austin asked.

"Right. The grass was trampled down and we found this shoe just lying there in the grass."

Austin reached over for the phone and dialed. He waited, then, said, "Let me talk to Dr. Severson, please."

"What are you calling him for?" Drollstrom inquired, confused why Austin wasn't excited about the find.

Ignoring Drollstrom, Austin waited for Severson to answer his call.

"Jerry," he said. "What size shoe did Arlis Upton wear? Yes, I'll hang on."

The room was quiet, waiting for Austin to continue his conversation. "Yes, I'm still here," he said after a minute or so. "Is that right? You're sure about that? Okay. What?"

Austin listened for a few more seconds and said, "Thanks, Jerry," and hung up the phone.

He threw the bag with the shoe over to Jacquie. "What size shoe is that?"

Jacquie looked at him, not sure what she was supposed to do. "You want me to open it?" she asked.

"Put a glove on first," Austin told her.

Jacquie reached into her pocket, pulled out a

glove, and put it on her right hand. She reached inside the bag and pulled out a black high heel shoe and checked the inside. "It's a size 6," she said. "She had small feet."

"No, she didn't," Austin said. "She wore a size 8½. That shoe isn't hers."

Austin took a sip of coffee and made a face. "This coffee sucks," he said. He glanced over where Sam Lober was standing. "We need to talk, Sam. In private."

"I was wondering when you'd get around to me," Sam told him.

"Now's as good a time as ever," Austin said, staring at Sam. "By the way, did you know that your girlfriend was pregnant?"

Sam looked Austin in the eyes. "Of course, I did," he said softly.

"Pete, I want you, Benny, and Matt to go back to where you found the shoe and continue looking for something – anything – that will give us an idea where Arlis went into the river."

Drollstrom looked at his watch. "It's almost quitting time."

"I don't think so," Austin replied. "There's no quitting time today. You search until it's dark, which will be around 8:30 or so. Got it? And, if you haven't finished up by then, I want you back out there first thing tomorrow morning. Understand?"

"Am I getting paid overtime for this?" Drollstrom asked, sarcastically.

"Jacquie, maybe you should go with them. You're in charge," Austin told her, ignoring

Drollstrom's question.

"Right," Jacquie said.

"There's no way she's in charge. I'm in charge of this search," Drollstrom whined.

"You were in charge," Austin said. "Now, you're not. You take your orders from Jacquie. Got it?"

"I don't take orders from a woman. You got that, Augie?" Drollstrom yelled.

Austin looked around, checking to be sure that no one had approached the dock. Satisfied that no one was watching, he checked the rope which was binding Drollstrom's wrists behind his back and determined that it was secure.

"You can't do this," Drollstrom yelled. "My father's the mayor."

Austin glanced down at the bucket of cement Drollstrom was standing in and laughed. "When they say quick-drying, they sure mean it," he uttered. "I'd say you're good to go."

"You're gonna be sorry. You'll never get away with this," Drollstrom cried out."

"Sure, I will," Austin told him and shoved him off the dock into the water. "Good riddance, you piece of shit," he muttered, as he watched Drollstrom disappear into the deep, dark water.

Chief Austin took a deep breath, got himself under control, looked Drollstrom in the eyes, and said, "That's Chief Austin to you. I want you out of here. Now!"

"Fuck you, Augie," Drollstrom screamed, as he

turned and left the room.

"What about my shift," Benny asked, after a few moments of silence. "I'm on at six."

"I'm filling in until you get back," Austin told him. "Now, everybody out."

Austin watched as Jacquie, Matt, and Benny scurried out of the room. He glanced over at Sam, who was pouring himself another cup of coffee. "Why didn't you tell me you were dating Arlis?" he asked.

Lober shrugged. "I messed up, didn't I?" he asked Austin.

"You did, Sam. Big time. Now, sit. We've got a lot to get to."

Chapter Fourteen

At eight-forty-five, Officer Benisch and Deputy Gorski were back at the station. Benisch walked in shaking his head. "Nothing," he said to Austin. "We didn't find a thing to indicate where Arlis was dumped."

Austin glanced up at Jacquie. "Jacquie?"

She shook her head no. "Benny's right. We've still got a few blocks to go, though. We decided to meet there at dawn tomorrow and finish up. But I'll tell you, Chief, it's not looking good, especially with the rain last night."

"Well, Pete did find that shoe," Benny remarked. "Who knows? We might get lucky tomorrow and actually find something useful."

"Tomorrow is Wednesday. She was killed Sunday night. I doubt there's anything there to find," Austin said.

"You're probably right, but we gotta keep searching. No stone left unturned. Right?" Benny said.

"Right," Austin replied.

"How'd it go with Sam?" Jacquie asked.

"About how I figured it would. He said he hasn't got a clue what happened to her," Austin told her.

"Has he got an alibi?" Jacquie inquired.

"He does. I still need to check it out, but it seems pretty solid. And, he did work his usual shift."

"So, he can account for his time from four a.m. to eight a.m. But where was he when Arlis was killed?" Jacquie asked.

"At home, in bed, and asleep. He said they went

to a church meeting from eight to around ten, he dropped Arlis off at her house right after, and he went home to bed."

"He still lives with his parents, doesn't he?"

"He does. I'm not really looking at him for her murder." He looked at Benny, who was listening to their conversation. "Are you good to work until midnight?" he asked him.

"I'm fine. Matt's gonna take midnight until eight. He went home to get some sleep."

"Alright, then. It seems you guys have everything covered. Jacquie, go home and get some sleep. Tomorrow is going to be a long day. Right now, I'm gonna go talk to Ronny Ott."

"We're looking for more than one killer, aren't we?" Jacquie asked. "These two cases don't have anything to do with each other, do they?"

Chief Austin shrugged, indicating he didn't know. "You may be right, Jacquie. At this point, I'm not sure. But I'm leaning that way. So far, nothing is connecting the two murders."

"Are you sure about Sam? That he's not involved, I mean," she asked.

"He's a strange one. His girlfriend gets murdered and he acts as if nothing has changed. He comes to work, does his job, and doesn't say a word. Even when I interviewed him, he didn't show hardly any emotion. In my book, that's not normal."

"Yet, you don't suspect him," Jacquie added.

"Not really. Like I said, I still need to check out his alibi. Now, go home."

"I'm going. There is one thing, though," she said,

hesitantly.

"What's that?" Austin asked.

"Well, Dr. Severson said it was hard to determine Arlis' exact time of death, with her being in the water so long."

"That's right. It could have been a little earlier or a little later. Midnight is an approximate time," Austin said.

"Do you think it could have been between four and eight in the morning?"

"I suppose it could have been. What are you getting at, Jacquie?" Austin asked.

Jacquie hesitated. "Forget it," she finally said.

"If you've got an idea, tell me," Austin said.

"It's just that once in a while. . ." She shook her head. "No, it's crazy."

"Jacquie?" Austin said, prompting her to finish her sentence. "Once in a while what?"

"Once in a while, Arlis rode with Sam while he was on duty. If she was killed later than midnight. . ."

"What the fuck, Jacquie?" Benny, yelled, interrupting her. "Whataya think you're doing, trying to pin this on Sam? There's no way in hell he would have hurt Arlis and you know it."

Jacquie glanced over at Benny and then looked away, embarrassed at what she had suggested. "You're right, Benny. I'm sorry. I guess I'm just tired and grasping at straws. Forget I said anything."

"Damned right, you're sorry," Benny said loudly.

"She's just doing her job, Benny," Austin told him. "We have to look at everybody until we find out who did this."

"Sit," Ronny Ott told him. "You want a beer?"

Austin looked around, trying to figure out where he could sit down. Clutter was piled up on every piece of furniture in the small living room, except for one large overstuffed chair.

Ronny grinned. "Guess this place could use a little cleaning."

"You think?" Austin said.

"Let's go in the kitchen and sit at the table."

Austin followed Ronny into the kitchen, expecting to see a total mess. However, he was surprised to see that the sink was empty of dirty dishes and the counter tops neat and clean.

Ronny grinned again, as he saw the surprised look on Austin's face. He reached into his refrigerator and pulled out a couple of Carling's Black Label beers. "I don't eat in the living room," he said. "I eat in here."

"I didn't say a word," Austin said, smiling.

"I figure you're here about Debbie Nelson," Ronny said, as he handed him a beer. "What do you need to know?"

Austin sat down at the table and took a swallow from the bottle. "This hits the spot," he commented. "It's been a long day."

"Well, you've got two murders on your hands. I figure all your days are gonna be long ones until you find out who murdered Debbie and Arlis."

"Tell me about you and Debbie," Austin said.

Three beers and an hour and ten minutes later, Austin shook hands with Ronny Ott and left his house.

He headed home, hoping that Catherine had kept his dinner warm. His stomach was growling for food and the three beers had gone straight to his head. Although the need for sleep was great, the need for food was overpowering.

He thought about why Ronny and Debbie had split up a little over six months ago. He liked the guy. Most men would be bad-mouthing an ex for cheating, but Ott talked about Debbie with respect. He had moved past his breakup with Debbie and indicated that he was seeing one of the Wendt girls. He seemed down to earth and extremely mature for someone who was only twenty-five. He owned the house he lived in on Water Street and was a self-employed plumber. He was the type of guy that Austin wished he had on the force. He seemed honest and dependable and Austin had believed everything he had said. Even so, he would still be checking out his alibi in the morning.

He yawned as he pulled into his driveway and turned off the ignition. Drollstrom flashed through his mind and he sighed as he thought of the conversation they would be having in the morning.

Chapter Fifteen

Pat McNally turned left off of Hwy. 60, drove a few hundred feet, made a right onto a gravel-covered driveway, and stopped. He looked over at the big old house, noting that there were lights on in the kitchen and living room. Good, he thought, the girls are here.

Not sure if it was going to rain, he opted on the side of caution and put the roof up on his turquoise Chevy Bel Air convertible. He smiled as a drop of rain bounced off of his forehead. Good timing, he thought, as he walked to the back of the house and entered the kitchen.

Sandra Peary was sitting at the table, smoking a cigarette. By the expression on her face, there was no doubt that she was upset. She turned and looked at Pat, then looked away.

"It just started to rain," Pat told her, smiling.

She gave him a disgusted look, and took a puff of her cigarette, blowing the smoke in his direction. "If I wanted to hear a weather forecast, I'd listen to the radio."

"Funny," Pat replied. "What are you so pissed about?"

"It's nine o'clock, Pat. Where are all our customers?"

"Are the rest of the girls here?" Pat asked. "I only saw one car out there."

"They're in the living room."

"Let's go join them, shall we? Grab me a beer, will you?"

Sandra got up from the table and gave him a

nasty look. "Get your own damn beer," she said and walked into the living room.

Annie and Rose were laughing at something that Karen had just told them. They glanced over at Sandra and Pat, saw the serious expressions on their faces, and immediately went quiet.

Pat stood in the doorway and looked at the three women. "What a beautiful sight," he said softly. "It almost hurts my eyes to gaze upon such beauty."

"Quit the crap, Pat," Sandra said, angrily. "What the hell is going on?'

"It does my heart good to know that you're all here, ready to work for dear old Pat. But, alas, I fear that it's time to close the doors."

"What the hell are you talking about?" yelled Annie, trying to be heard over the shouting of the other three women.

Suddenly, a shrill whistle filled the air and everyone looked at Sandra. "Everyone be quiet," she said. "Pat has some explaining to do. Don't you Pat?"

Pat, still standing in the doorway, smiled at her. "Indeed, I do. But, first, you lovely ladies, I'm getting myself a beer," he said. "Can I get you anything?"

"Why are you talking like that?" Rose asked, a confused look on her face.

It didn't take long for Pat to explain his plan to the four women. It didn't take long for them to agree. It was a good plan. It solved their money problems and got them off their backs. If this worked, their whoring days were over.

Two hours later, the four women – a little high

and undoubtedly drunk - climbed into Sandra's car and drove off.

Pat McNally was also a little high and just a little sad as he walked through the old farmhouse. He'd done well here. He'd made a lot of money – thanks to the five needy friends who had whored for him – but it was time to cut bait. He had heard that Austin was asking around town about a whore house. It was time to move on to something else before Austin started putting two and two together.

If that damned Debbie had just stayed away from all that S&M shit, they'd still be in business. He should have known that someday it would get out of hand and someone would get hurt. They got too greedy – him and Debbie – and she lost her life because of it.

He wasn't worried that the 'John' who had killed her would be found. Even if someone looked down that old dried-up well, all they'd see is a bunch of rocks. He was confident that the guy's body would be entombed forever. His biggest mistake was not dumping Debbie in after him.

They'd had a pretty good run of it and made a lot of money. He wasn't concerned about the women talking. They were partners in crime. He knew what the women had done. They knew what he had done. In a day or two, this old wooden farmhouse, which held so many secrets, would go up in flames. He'd collect the insurance, pay off the girls so they could open their restaurant, and that would be the end of it.

As Pat stumbled into the kitchen to get another beer, he didn't notice that the back door was slightly ajar.

Officer Pete Drollstrom followed Sandra when she headed out of town on Hwy. 60. He passed the side road she turned off on, did a u-turn, and parked on the side of the highway. He watched the four women get out of the car and go into a farmhouse. He was still watching the house when Pat McNally pulled into the driveway, put the top up on his car, and went inside. Drollstrom sat for the next few hours and drank a few beers, keeping an eye on the house. He started to nod off a few times but was wide awake when the four women, obviously drunk, crawled into Sandra's car and drove off. He debated going after them. He could probably arrest Sandra for drunk driving but decided against it.

He had heard the rumors that McNally was running a cat house, but no other cars had shown up. Right now, it looked like they had just had a small party and nothing suspicious had gone on. Besides, he wasn't on duty and he didn't want to show his hand by letting them know he had been watching them. He wondered if McNally was screwing one of them. Hell, knowing McNally like he did, he figured good old Pat was probably fucking all of them.

Suddenly, a shot rang out, disturbing the noisy chirps of crickets that were looking for a mate. Drollstrom, not sure where the shot came from, exited his car and looked in the direction of the farmhouse. When a second shot filled the air, he knew it was coming from the farm.

He jumped back into his car and drove the short

distance to the house. Throwing the car into park, he jumped out yelling, "Police!" He reached down and pulled a gun out of his ankle holster, yelled police again, and ducked down behind the open car door.

A third shot bounced off the gravel next to the open car door, scaring him, and causing him to fall backward. More angry than frightened, he stood, aimed at a figure running towards him from the back of the house, and fired.

"What the fuck!"

"Drop your gun," Drollstrom yelled.

"What the fuck, man! You shot me," McNally shouted. "Quit shooting. What the hell is wrong with you?"

"Drop your gun! Now!" Drollstrom yelled again.

"Alright," McNally yelled and dropped his rifle onto the ground.

"You're under arrest for attempted murder, McNally," Drollstrom shouted at him.

"Are you fucking nuts? I wasn't trying to kill you. I didn't even know you were here. You shot me, you idiot."

"You shot at me first."

"I was shooting at a fucking raccoon that got in my house," McNally told him.

"Right. Like I believe that story," Drollstrom said.

"I give a shit if you believe it or not. That's what happened. What the hell are you doing here, anyway?"

The seriousness of the situation hit Drollstrom like a ton of bricks. He had just shot a man. How the hell was he going to explain this screw-up to Austin?

"Where are you hit?" he asked McNally, as he

81

reached down and holstered his weapon.

"My leg. The right one." McNally moaned. "Damn, it really hurts. Do you think you could run in and get some towels? They're in a drawer in the kitchen," McNally said, as he slowly dropped down onto the gravel driveway.

Drollstrom ran past McNally and headed for the kitchen, trying to figure out how he was going to get out of this mess.

Chapter Sixteen

"You've known me for a long time, right?" Pete Drollstrom asked Pat McNally.

McNally glanced over at him. "Since kindergarten. Why?"

"We've always gotten along pretty good, haven't we?"

"I guess. Where are you going with this, Pete?"

Drollstrom slowed down a little, checked to be sure there was no traffic approaching the intersection, hit the gas, and sped through the stop light. The hospital was just at the top of the hill and the closer they got the more worried he became. "How about I drop you off at the door? There's no reason anyone has to know I accidentally shot you. You could say you shot yourself while cleaning your gun."

McNally grinned. "Why would I do that? Are you afraid you're gonna get in trouble?"

"Hey, man, it was an accident. You know that. But I could lose my job over this or even worse. I don't see anything funny about it."

"I thought you couldn't be fired. At least, that's what I heard."

"I can't. Not for the small stuff. But this is different. If you tell anyone that I shot you, I could go to jail or something."

"Or something? Like what?"

"I don't know, man. It's just that - well - I don't know. Can you keep this between us?"

"What's in it for me?"

Drollstrom glanced over at him. "What do you

83

mean?"

"I mean, Pete, what do I get out of it?"

Drollstrom made a left onto Lewis St. and stopped in front of the hospital. He turned and looked straight at McNally. "Anything you want. I'll owe you one."

McNally laughed. "One? Do you think this is a one-favor deal? If I agree to this, you're mine, Pete. Got it?"

"Come on, man," Drollstrom whined. "It was an accident."

"You fucking shot me!" McNally declared, raising his voice. "You could have killed me and now you want me to do you a favor?"

"The doctor has to report a gunshot wound and, if you tell them I shot you, I'll have a lot of explaining to do. Even if it was an accident."

"I need to get in there. This leg is bleeding like a stuck pig. Drive me up to the door."

"What are you gonna tell them?" Pete asked.

"I'm not sure."

"Please, Pat. I'm begging you. Don't say anything."

McNally hesitated before answering him. "I'll keep you out of it. For now. But you owe me big time, Pete. I mean it."

Pete pulled the car up to the hospital door and waited until Pat managed to get out of the car. "Thanks, man," he yelled, as he hit the gas pedal and took off, leaving Pat to hobble into the hospital by himself.

At eight o'clock Wednesday morning, Chief Austin received a telephone call from the head nurse at Columbus Community Hospital. She informed him that around eleven-thirty, the previous night, Pat McNally had checked himself in to be treated for a gunshot wound to the leg. She said that Dr. Poszert had been called in and an operation had been performed to remove the bullet and dress the wound.

"Is he there now?" Austin asked the nurse.

"No, he's not. He checked himself out a few hours after Dr. Poszert removed the bullet," she said.

"Did he say who shot him?"

"As I understand it, it was self-inflicted. He said he accidentally shot himself while he was cleaning his gun."

"I'll need to talk to him," Austin said.

"According to his records, he called a friend to pick him up and take him home. Do you need his address?" the nurse asked.

"Thanks, but I know where he lives. I assume you have the bullet," Austin stated. "I'll be over to pick it up sometime today."

"Hold on a minute," the nurse said and laid the phone down. Austin could hear her talking to someone, but couldn't make out what she was saying.

"Are you still there?" she asked Austin when she came back on the line.

"I'm here," he replied.

"He took the bullet with him," the nurse told Austin.

"What do you mean, he took it with him? He can't just take the bullet. You know when there's a shooting, I need to check it out and that bullet is part of the investigation," Austin shouted.

"Don't raise your voice at me. I wasn't here last night. I guess Dr. Poszert wasn't thinking straight. It was late and maybe he was tired. Anyway, the night nurse just told me that Pat wanted it as a souvenir, and Dr. Poszert gave it to him. Sorry."

"Damn!" Austin exclaimed and immediately apologized. "Sorry, I shouldn't have said that."

"That's okay, Augie. I've heard worse than that. Do you need anything else? I've got patients to check on."

"Not for now," Austin told her.

"Call me if I can help you with anything else."

Pat McNally opened the door and smiled. "Good morning, Pete. How are you this fine morning?"

Pete glared at him. "What the hell are you so happy about?"

"I'm doing fine. Thanks for asking," Pat replied.

"Sorry. I didn't get much sleep last night and I'm already late for work, which means Austin will be pissed and I'm not in the mood to be yelled at. What do you want, anyway?"

"I want to talk to you."

"What's so important that you couldn't talk to me over the phone?"

"I have a favor to ask."

Pete looked at him like he had lost his mind. "You what?"

"I need a favor."

"Look, Pat, I know I said I'd do anything if you

kept quiet about me shooting you, but I've changed my mind. I don't want to be in debt to you. After all, you're not hurt that bad, and besides, you can't prove I shot you. You already told the doctor that you shot yourself. So, how about we just forget about the whole thing?"

Pat hobbled to a chair and sat down. He stared at Pete, not saying anything.

"So, are we good?" Pete asked, starting to feel nervous.

Pat smiled. "You never told me what you were doing at my place last night, Pete. Just why were you there?"

"I was just driving by when I heard some shots and I pulled in to see if I could help."

"I see. You were driving down the highway and you just happened to be right there while I was shooting at a raccoon? You weren't there spying on me?"

Pete looked shocked. "Of course not. Why would I be doing that?"

"You tell me," Pat said softly. "Tell me the real reason why you were there."

"I just told you."

"I don't believe you, Pete. Why don't you sit down? We've got a lot to talk about."

"I've got to get going."

"Sit!" Pat yelled.

Pete jumped at the sound. "Fuck you, Pat. I'm out of here."

"Sit your ass down. Now!" Pat ordered him.

"I'm not doing you any favors. Forget it," Pete

yelled.

"Yes, you are. And, it's gonna be today."

"Today?" Pete looked puzzled. "You want a favor already?"

"That's right."

"What the hell is it?"

"I want you to burn my house down."

Pete stared at him. "This house?"

Pat laughed. "No, you idiot. I live here. I want you to torch the farmhouse. Tonight."

"Why do you want to burn it down?"

"You don't need to know. Tonight, after dark – let's say ten or so – I want you to burn it down."

Pete shook his head. "I'm not burning your fucking house down. Are you crazy?"

Pat sighed. "You have a choice, Pete. Either you do what I ask or I'll call your father and tell him you shot me. And, of course, I'll call Chief Austin. I'm sure he will be very interested in knowing that you were sneaking around my place last night and, for no reason at all, you shot me. That just might be the ammunition he needs to finally get rid of you."

"No way, man. Forget it. It's your word against mine. And, if you say anything, I'll tell them that you asked me to burn your house down."

"You discharged your weapon and didn't report it. I believe that's a crime, seeing as how you're a cop. You shot me without any provocation. I think that's a crime, also. You were trespassing on my property last night. I'm not sure if that is a crime, but I think it might be."

Pete smirked, as he listened to Pat. "Like I said,

man, it's your word against mine."

"No, Pete, it isn't. I've got the proof."

"What proof?"

"You mean besides my blood in your car?

Pete glared at him. "Ya, besides that. Because I already cleaned the inside of my car."

"There's no way you got it all. But that isn't even important. I've got the bullet. Now, sit your ass down so we can go over the plans for tonight."

Chapter Seventeen

Chief Austin pulled his car over to the curb and parked in front of Pat McNally's house. He glanced over at the three cars parked in his driveway and frowned. He had wanted McNally to be alone when he questioned him about the shooting, but it was obvious that wasn't going to happen

As he exited his squad car, he could hear Elvis' latest hit, Teddy Bear, playing inside the house. God, I hate that song, Austin thought as he walked up to the front door and rang the doorbell. He waited, realized that Pat probably couldn't hear the bell over the music, and yelled, "Pat, it's Chief Austin. I need to talk to you."

He put his nose to the screen, trying to see inside, and waited. Frustrated over not being heard, Austin opened the door and walked into Pat's house. He looked around and realized that voices were coming from the kitchen. "Pat!" he yelled. "It's Chief Austin. I'm coming in."

Just as he was about to step into the kitchen, Sandra Peary came through the doorway, blocking his entry. "Chief," she said, giving him a big smile. "What brings you here?"

Austin smiled back at her. "It's a little early to be having a party, don't you think?" he practically yelled.

Sandra gave him a questioning look. "Sorry, I can't hear you."

Austin looked around the living room, spotted the record player, walked over to it, and turned it off. "That's better," he declared. "I couldn't hear myself think with that noise blaring."

"Don't you just love that song?" Sandra asked him. "I could listen to it all day long."

"Sorry, but I can't say I do. It seems that it's the only thing my daughter listens to these days. I'm afraid Elvis is starting to get on my nerves."

Sandra laughed. "Well, I love him. I doubt he could ever get on my nerves. Are you here to see Pat?" she asked him.

"I am. I gather he's in the kitchen."

"He is. We stopped over to make sure he was okay. Would you care for a cup of coffee?"

Austin smiled. "I think I've had my fill of coffee for today. But I could use a glass of cold water."

"Coming up," Sandra said, motioning for him to follow her into the kitchen.

"Well, look who's here," Pat said, as Austin stuck his head in the doorway and looked into the room.

"Is it safe to come in?" Austin asked.

"You know what they say - the more the merrier," Pat told him. "However, the ladies were just leaving."

"Good morning," Austin said, acknowledging Annie, Karen, and Rose. "Good to see you again." He hesitated for a second, and then added, "I just heard that Debbie Nelson's funeral will be on Friday at two o'clock."

No one said anything.

"I need to talk to you, Pat," Austin said, breaking the silence.

"Of course," Pat replied. "Ladies," he said softly, "I'll see you later. Thanks for stopping by."

He waited until they had left the room, then, turned to Austin. "I think we might be more comfortable in the living room."

While Pat made himself comfortable on the couch, Austin checked out the living room. It was furnished nicely, with a matching couch and chair and a couple of end tables. Austin took a seat in the overstuffed chair and faced Pat. "Are you okay?" he asked.

"It hurts a little, but nothing I can't handle. Of course, I have pain pills if I need them, but so far I've managed without them."

"How did it happen?"

"You mean, how did I shoot myself?"

"That's exactly what I mean, Pat. You're a hunter. You've been around guns all your life. It seems a little strange that you would be so careless while cleaning a gun."

Pat looked embarrassed. "You're right. I was careless. I didn't realize the gun was loaded. I never leave a loaded gun in the house, so I assumed it was empty. I didn't check it."

"I need the bullet and your rifle," Austin said.

"What for?"

"I need to check the bullet against your rifle. It's just routine, but it needs to be done. Rules, you know. They have to be followed."

"Well, I don't have the bullet."

Austin looked surprised. "I was told that Dr. Poszert gave it to you. Are you saying that didn't happen?"

"No. I'm saying I don't have it. I lost it."

Austin stared at Pat, trying to decide if he was lying. "And, when was the last time you saw it?"

"When I put it in my pocket. But it must have fallen out."

"It fell out?" Austin inquired.

Pat smiled. "They cut my pants leg off at the hospital. I didn't realize that they had cut part of the pocket off at the same time. When they gave me the bullet, I slipped it into my pocket. I guess it fell out somewhere."

"So, you have no idea where you lost it?"

"All I know is that when I reached into my pocket to get it, it wasn't there. I have no idea where or when it fell out," Pat told him.

Austin sat back in his chair and frowned. "You do realize that Dr. Poszert should never have given it to you, don't you?"

Pat shrugged. "How would I know that? It seems to me that you should discuss that with Poszert."

Austin stood up. "Right. I'll be off, then. If you find that bullet, will you give me a call?"

Pat smiled. "Of course."

"Can I get you anything before I leave?" Austin asked him.

"A new leg would be nice," Pat said, laughing.

Chapter Eighteen

"What are you so upset about?" Jacquie asked Austin. "You've been pacing the room for the past twenty minutes."

Austin stopped and looked at her. "I've wasted this entire morning and I'm no closer to finding out who murdered those women than I was two days ago."

"How did it go with Pat McNally this morning? Did you get the bullet?" Jacquie asked.

"That's the other thing," Austin said, raising his voice. "He said he lost it."

"You don't believe him?" Jacquie inquired.

"Not for a minute."

"Why not? Why would he lie about it?"

Austin stared at her and sighed. "I don't have any idea. Maybe, he is telling the truth. I just get the feeling that something is going on with that guy. And, who do you think was there when I got to his house?"

Jacquie shrugged. "I have no idea."

"Those four friends of Debbie Nelson's, that's who. The music was so loud they didn't even hear the doorbell. It was like they were having a celebration or something. I tell you, Jacquie, there's something fishy about those four women. I just can't put my finger on it."

"Are you talking about Karen, Rose, Annie, and Sandra?"

Austin shook his head yes. "Debbie isn't even in the ground yet, and they act like nothing happened. That isn't the way friends should act, for crying out loud."

94

"I know the Nelsons are good friends with you and Mrs. Austin, so is it possible that you're being more sensitive about this than usual?" Jacquie asked him.

Austin walked over to his desk and sat down. "Maybe, you're right. I'm at a loss here, Jacquie."

"Let's review what we've got," Jacquie said. "Let's start at the beginning and work through it again. I don't know about you, but I still think that Arlis' death has nothing to do with what happened to Debbie. I think we have two separate cases and two killers."

"I think you're right. Why don't you lay it all out and we'll go over everything when I get back?"

"Where are you going?" Jacquie asked.

"First I'm going to see Rev. Albrecht and then I'm going to go talk to Sam Lober."

"He's probably sleeping."

"Then I'll wake him up."

Sam Lober answered the door, wearing only his boxers. His hair was a mess and he had sleep creases on his face. He looked surprised when he saw Chief Austin standing at the door.

"Looks like I woke you," Austin commented.

"You did. What's up?"

"Can I come in? I need to talk to you."

Sam pushed the door open all the way so that Austin could enter the house. He led him into the living room. "You want something to drink?" he muttered, rubbing his eyes.

"I'm fine, thanks. Are your parents here, Sam?"

"Na. They're at work."

"I want you to go over everything that you and Arlis did the night she was murdered. Go slow and don't leave anything out."

Sam looked a little confused. "I already told you everything."

"Tell me again."

"We had dinner here, with my folks."

"What time was that?" Austin asked.

"Around five-thirty or so. We talked for a while and then Arlis and I went to a meeting at the church."

"What church?"

"The Lutheran Church," Sam answered.

"On Mill Street?"

"It's the only Lutheran church in town," Sam said.

"Go on," Austin prompted.

"After the meeting was over, which was around ten, I dropped Arlis off at her place, I went home, and I went to bed."

"And, you didn't see her after that?" Austin asked.

"No. That was the last time I saw her."

"How did you feel about her being pregnant? Did it upset you?"

"It did. I loved her, but I wasn't ready to get married and have a kid," Sam answered, raising his voice a little.

"So, it upset you that she was pregnant?

"Maybe a little," Sam said. "But, not enough to kill her, if that's what you're getting at."

"How often did Arlis ride with you when you were on patrol?"

96

Sam's head jerked up and he glanced over at Austin, his face turning red. "What do you mean?" he said, looking away.

"Exactly what I said. How often?"

"It was only a few times," Sam said, after a few seconds.

"When was the last time?"

"A few weeks ago, I guess. You know I work a lot. I didn't have as much time as I wanted to spend with her, so sometimes she rode with me."

Austin didn't say anything.

"It didn't hurt anything. Nothing much happens between four and eight in the morning. You know that. It gave us a chance to spend a little more time together." He looked up at Austin. "I'm sorry. It was wrong."

"It was wrong, Sam. I'd be lying if I said I wasn't disappointed in you. I heard that you and Arlis fought the night she was murdered. What were you fighting about?"

"That's a damned lie," Sam said, angrily. "Who told you that?"

"Rev. Albrecht, Sam. He said you two started arguing about something at the meeting. What were you fighting about?"

"We weren't really fighting. It was more like a disagreement. It was nothing."

"You said you left the church meeting around ten. Is that correct?"

Sam looked at Austin, wondering how much he knew. "It might have been a little earlier."

"Maybe you didn't stay for the whole meeting.

Maybe you left at least an hour before it ended."

Sam didn't respond to Austin's comments.

"Sam, why don't you tell me what really happened? Where did you and Arlis go between the time you left the church and dropped her off at her house?"

"Nowhere. We didn't go anyplace. We sat in the car and talked."

"You talked or you argued?" Austin asked.

"Talked. We talked."

"What about?"

Sam put his hands in his face, fighting to hold back the tears. "Nothing," he muttered.

"Tell me, Sam."

He took his hands away and looked straight into Austin's eye. "Arlis and I never had sex. The baby wasn't mine."

Austin sat back in his chair, totally surprised at what Sam had just told him. He looked at the tears filling Sam's eyes, trying to understand the pain he was going through.

"I'm so sorry," Austin said softly.

"I didn't kill her!" Sam yelled. "It wasn't her I was angry with and I didn't kill her. You have to believe me."

"Who were you angry with if it wasn't Arlis?"

Sam shrugged and looked away.

"This doesn't look good for you, Sam. You lied to me. You were the last person to see Arlis alive."

"I wasn't the last person. Whoever killed her was the last person who saw her, and that wasn't me. I loved her. I would never have hurt her."

"Did Arlis tell you who the father was?"

"No. But, if she had, that's who this town would be burying Friday and not her. She was raped, Chief. Her unborn child was the result of that assault."

"Ah, shit, Sam. Damn it all, anyway." Austin stood up and looked out the living room window. "How did you leave it with her?" he asked Sam.

"I'm not proud of this, but we decided that she should get an abortion."

Austin turned and stared at Sam. "You know that's illegal, don't you?"

"I know. We heard about a place in Madison that does them. We talked about going there."

"Who was going to pay for it? I understand they cost a pretty penny."

"I guess. We hadn't got that far with our plans, yet. Arlis said she wanted to get the money from the guy that raped her, but I told her to stay away from him."

"And, she never told you his name?"

"No, she wouldn't tell me."

"Maybe, she did ask for money," Austin speculated. "Maybe the same person who raped her is the one who killed her."

"You think?" Sam asked.

"It's possible that she threatened to tell if he didn't give her the money. That would have been a motive to get rid of her," Austin said.

"I miss her so much, Chief. I should have married her and let her have the baby. It's just that I couldn't stand the thought of raising a child. . ."

Austin was quiet as Sam put his face in his

hands and sobbed.

"If I hadn't insisted that she. . . that she get rid of it. . . she'd be alive. It's all my fault," Sam said, barely able to speak.

Austin reached down and picked his hat up from the coffee table. He bent down and put his hand on Sam's shoulder, squeezing it. "I'm so sorry, Sam. Let me know if there's anything I can do."

"I appreciate it, Chief. I really do. But the only thing I need for you to do is to find the son of a bitch that did this and give me ten minutes alone with him."

The minute Austin was back at the police station, he went to his desk, picked up the phone, and dialed Dr. Severson. Jacquie started to ask him a question, but he motioned for her to be quiet.

"Jerry," he said, "what did you do with the fetus from the Upton woman?"

Chapter Nineteen

"Why?"

"I want you to run a paternity test," Austin told Dr. Severson.

"Against who?"

"I don't know, yet. But I've got to find out who fathered that baby. Arlis Upton was raped. Whoever did it is the father of that baby."

"No shit. I'm sorry to hear that. The best I can do is take samples of blood from Arlis and the fetus and preserve them until you get a suspect. Other than that, there's no way to determine who the father is. Jones' Funeral Home is picking up her body this afternoon. A few more hours and it would have been too late to get a blood sample. I've still got the fetus. I was just about to dispose of it and you know where that goes. It's a good thing you called me when you did."

"Thanks, Jerry," Austin said. "By the way, is there anything new on Debbie Nelson?"

"You've got it all," the medical examiner told him.

"Right. I'll talk to you later," Austin said and hung up the phone.

Jacquie gazed at him, wondering what was happening. Austin looked over at her and frowned. "We have a rapist in town. Can you fucking believe that?"

Jacquie sat back in her chair, looking shocked. "What the hell are you talking about?" she asked.

"Arlis Upton was raped. That baby she was

carrying wasn't Sam's."

"No way! Do you know who raped her?"

"No. But, I sure as hell intend to find out."

"Probably the same person who killed her," Jacquie commented.

"Most likely. By the way, call Matt and see if he can work Sam's shift tonight."

"Sam's not coming in?"

"No. I told him to stay home for the rest of the week. He's pretty shook up, Jacquie. He blames himself for Arlis' death."

"Why would he do that? He didn't kill her."

Austin got up and put his index finger to his mouth, indicating that Jacquie should be quiet. He slowly moved to the door and swung it open. Officer Pete Drollstrom jumped back, a surprised look on his face.

"What the hell! You scared me," Drollstrom yelled, his face turning bright red, embarrassed at being caught listening at the door.

"Exactly how long have you been standing out here listening, Pete?" Austin asked.

"I just got here," Drollstrom replied.

"Really? You didn't hear anything?"

"Not really. Just that Sam's in bad shape. I'm sorry to hear that."

"Get in here," Austin said sharply and walked back to his desk.

Drollstrom sauntered into the room, like he didn't have a care in the world, and sat down at his desk.

"Where have you been all morning?" Jacquie

asked him.

"Doing my job, that's where. Besides, what's it to you?"

"Where have you been?" Austin asked him. "I'd like to know, since this is the first time I've seen you this morning."

"It's afternoon," Drollstrom said, sarcastically.

"What?" Austin asked.

"It's after twelve o'clock. That makes it afternoon, not morning."

"Are you being a smart ass?"

"No," Drollstrom replied. "Just setting the facts straight."

"God, give me strength," Jacquie uttered.

"Would you like to tell me what you've been doing for the past four and a half hours?" Austin said softly, trying to hold back his temper.

"If you insist," Drollstrom said, smugly.

"I do."

Suddenly, Drollstrom jumped up and reached into his pocket. "Da da," he sang out, as he pulled out a small evidence bag and held it up.

Jacquie and Austin glanced at it, then, looked at each other, wondering what was going on.

"I think I've solved your murder case," Drollstrom told them.

"Really? Which murder case? Arlis or Debbie?" Austin asked.

"Arlis."

"What's in the bag?" Jacquie inquired.

"I walked the river bank again. That's what I've been doing. I wanted to be sure we didn't miss

103

anything and – wait for it – guess. . ."

"Knock it off, Pete," Austin shouted. "If you found something, just say so."

"You're no fun. You know that, Augie?" Drollstrom declared.

"It's Chief Austin, Pete."

"Whatever." Drollstrom reached into the bag and pulled out a cigarette lighter and tossed it to Austin. "What do you think of that?" he asked.

Austin looked at it and frowned. "Where did you find this?"

Drollstrom grinned. "You know who that belongs to, don't you?" he asked, ignoring Austin's question.

"I do. It's Sam's lighter. Where did you find it?"

"It was lying in the grass behind the canning factory. I figure that's where Sam threw her in and her body got hung up on that tree branch almost as soon as she was tossed into the river. It looks like Sam's your guy."

"The lighter was behind the canning factory, Jacquie," Austin said. "What do you think of that?"

Jacquie stared at Drollstrom, a disgusted look on her face. "I think Pete is a fucking liar," she said. "That's what I think."

"I have to agree," Austin said. "Do you think I should arrest him for lying, planting evidence in an attempt to frame a fellow officer, and obstruction of justice?"

"Is that all?" Jacquie asked. "Surely, you can find a few more laws that he's broken."

Drollstrom watched the exchange between Austin and Jacquie, wondering what was going on. He had just handed them proof that Sam probably killed Arlis and they were talking about arresting him. "I'm not lying," he yelled. "What's wrong with you guys?"

"Sit down, Pete," Austin said and waited until Pete was in his chair.

"What?"

"Did you know that Sam quit smoking?"

Jacquie smiled as she watched Pete squirm in his chair.

"So?" Drollstrom asked.

"So, Pete, I had his lighter. He gave it to me a few weeks ago. He said he didn't have any use for it anymore."

Drollstrom looked away and didn't say anything.

"Pete, I figure there are only two ways that lighter could have made its way to the river. One is if it grew legs and walked there. I'm pretty sure that didn't happen. So, I figure that someone took it out of my desk drawer and pretended to find it by the river. Someone, who wants to be the big-shot policeman who solved Arlis' murder, even if it means framing his fellow officer. Am I right, Pete? Is that what happened?"

"You don't know what you're talking about," Drollstrom yelled. "I found it exactly where I said I did. You just don't want me to get the credit. You're just jealous because I'm a better cop than you are."

"Pete, Pete, Pete. What is wrong with you?" Jacquie said, shaking her head. "You really need to get some help."

Austin saw him walking down the dark, lonely

105

road. It wouldn't be an accident. It would be premeditated murder. He had been waiting for this opportunity for weeks.

He hit the gas, looked down at his speedometer, and had his car up to 65 mph when he struck Drollstrom, propelling his body into the air. He hit the brakes, did a uey, and gunned it, driving over the bloody body lying in the middle of the road.

Laughing, Austin turned the car around again and ran over the body for the second time. He stopped, tempted to get out of his car and check the body. No need, he thought. No one could have survived that.

Smiling, he drove off, thinking how good a root beer float would taste before he went home to Catherine and the kids.

"You know what?" Pete yelled. "I don't need this shit! Just what do you think is gonna happen when I inform my father what you just accused me of? You went too far this time, Augie."

Jacquie, who was watching Austin, turned to Pete. "I seriously think you should get out of here, Pete," she said. "You made a big mistake doing what you just did, with that lighter and all. However, I think you should leave while Chief Austin settles down. For some reason, I have a feeling that he is about to blow and I don't think you should be here when it happens."

"Ya, well, you know what I . . ."

"Pete," Jacquie yelled. "Get the hell out of here. Now!"

Drollstrom gave her a dirty look, got up, and left

the room.

"I'm going to lunch," she told Austin and followed Drollstrom out the door.

Chapter Twenty

"Thanks for coming back," Pat McNally said. "I was starving." He took the wrapping off the hamburger and took a huge bite. "Just the way I like it."

Sandra Peary watched him swallow the mouthful of food and smiled. "You should chew your food a little more. You practically swallowed that whole."

"Like I said, I was starving. There's nothing in this house to eat."

"How about I go grocery shopping for you? I've got to pick up a few things for myself, anyway. It's no problem. Make a list of what you need."

"Thanks, Sandra. I'd go myself, but I'm still a little shaky on this leg."

"I still can't believe that idiot shot you," Sandra said, laughing. "What an ass he is."

"It's not funny," Pat said, grinning. "Although, I. . ." He hesitated for a moment.

"What?" Sandra said, prompting him to finish his thought.

"I still don't know why he was there. It's just a feeling, but I think he was spying on me."

"You think he knows what's been going on out there?" Sandra inquired.

"I'm not sure." Pat shrugged. "I guess it doesn't make any difference now. I own his ass. He knows better than to say anything."

"I don't trust him. Are you sure he'll burn your house tonight?"

"He better, if he knows what's good for him."

"What time tonight?"

"Around ten."

"I'd like to see it," Sandra told him.

"You can't. You need to be here with me. You are going to be my alibi."

"Really?" Sandra said. "Are you asking me or telling me?"

Pat laughed. "Asking, darlin'. I know better than to tell you to do something."

"When do you think we'll get the insurance money?"

"I'm not sure. I've been thinking about it and. . ."

"What?" Sandra interrupted. "What about it?"

Pat, noting the anxiety in her voice, reached over and took her hand. "I have a better deal for you, Sandra."

Sandra pulled her hand away and stared at him. "What the hell, Pat? Are you backing out of our agreement? You promised us that money."

"Relax, will you?"

"What deal are you talking about?" Sandra stood up and started pacing back and forth. "I should have known we couldn't trust you. Shit, Pat, you're ruining everything."

"Listen to me, will you?" Pat said, raising his voice. "Sit down and let me tell you what I'm thinking."

Sandra glared at him. "Maybe, I should just leave."

"Damn it, Sandra. Listen to me, will you?"

"What?"

"Did you know that The Country Inn is up for sale again?"

"So? We can't afford that place."

"You can if I come in as a partner. If we combine our assets, we can afford it. You wouldn't need to get a loan and we'd own it lock, stock, and barrel."

"Are you serious?" Sandra asked. "How big a share do you want?"

"That's the thing. I don't want much from the restaurant profits. We'll have to work that out. But I get all the profits from the motel."

Sandra looked confused. "What motel?"

"I want to build a motel next to the restaurant. Right now, people have to go to Beaver Dam or Sun Prairie if they need a place to stay. Columbus is growing and it could use a small motel here. You can feed them and I'll give them a place to sleep."

Sandra sat back in her chair, thinking about what Pat had just said. "I'll have to pass it by the others," she said.

"You know as well as I do that if you agree to this, they'll go along with it."

"I'm just not sure if we want a restaurant that's out of town. I know it's only a mile or so, but we want to open a family place. The Country Inn's prices have always been a little steep. I don't know if we'd pull in families."

"Sandra, you're not thinking outside the box. You can have any kind of restaurant you want. It won't be The Country Inn anymore. It will be anything you want it to be. We'll gut it and you can start from scratch. You can make it into your family-friendly restaurant. Hell, you can put a sandbox in the entry and a playground out in front, if that's what you want."

"I don't understand why you want to do this. It doesn't sound like you are getting much out of it for what it's going to cost you."

"I'm selling the farm. The land is valuable and I'm sure it will sell fast. I'll need to invest the money in something and I think this will work. With what I'll get from the insurance company, the sale of the farm, and the money you guys have stashed away, we'll be in good shape. Like I said, we'll be debt-free and have no loan to pay back."

Sandra was quiet, thinking about Pat's offer.

"Well?" Pat asked, breaking the silence. "What do you think?"

"You fucker!" Sandra suddenly cried out. "You rotten fucker!"

Pat sat back, surprised by her outburst. "What?"

"You're going to build a motel? I know you, Pat, and I know what you've got up your sleeve. That's no motel you want to build. It's a cat house, isn't it?"

Pat grinned from ear to ear. "Okay. You got me. The thought did cross my mind."

"You understand that we're done whoring for you, don't you? Those days are over."

"Not a problem."

"Really?" Sandra asked, suspiciously.

"It actually will be a motel," Pat said. "At least half – maybe four or five rooms -will be run just like any other normal motel. The rest of the rooms will be money-makers. I should get my investment back in no time."

"What about girls? You certainly can't go local."

"That won't be a problem. And, no, they won't be local. Hell, I can walk down any street in Madison and find a dozen women ready to lie on their backs for a buck. Anyway, by the time the motel is ready for business, people will have forgotten the rumor going around town about a whorehouse somewhere in the area. People have short memories. That rumor will be long forgotten."

"And, we can change the restaurant to make it family-friendly? We can do whatever we want?"

"Sandra, you have full control over that end of the business and as soon as we close the deal, you can start doing your thing. I figure you'll be open for business in a couple of months. The motel will take longer, of course, being new construction and all. But the way I see it, you should be able to open the restaurant by Christmas."

"I can't believe it," Sandra said, as she reached over and hugged Pat. "My dreams are really going to come true."

Pat slid his hand under her blouse and gently squeezed her left breast. "You have the nicest tits," he said, as he reached around and unhooked her bra.

"Seriously, Pat? In the middle of the day?"

Pat grinned. "Why not," he uttered softly, as he reached down and unzipped his pants. Now, let's make one of my dreams come true, shall we?"

Chapter Twenty-one

"You're gonna do what?" Ronny Ott exclaimed. "Are you fucking nuts?"

"Quiet down, Ronny," Drollstrom whispered. "You're too loud." He looked around the bar, checking to see if anyone was listening to their conversation. "I don't have much of a choice, do I? He'll tell Austin I shot him if I don't do it."

"You're crazy, you know. How can you even think about burning his house down? You're a cop, Pete, in case you forgot."

Drollstrom shrugged. "What do you think I should do, then?"

Ronny Ott thought about it for a few seconds and then shook his head. "I don't have a fucking idea. Maybe, you should talk to Austin. Tell him what's going on."

"You know I can't do that. I'm already in trouble with him."

"What did you do now?"

Drollstrom looked over at him, deciding if he should tell him about the lighter. "Forget it. It was nothing."

"Hey, I'm your best friend. You can tell me anything."

"I said it was nothing."

"Alright. Don't get your underwear in a bunch. So, why don't you tell him about McNally's cathouse? That should get you off the hook."

"I can't do it. I don't have any proof. I'm pretty sure that's what he's been using that old farmhouse for, but I can't prove it. Why do you think he wants me to burn it down?"

"Probably for the insurance money."

"Could be, I guess. You went with Debbie for a long time, Ronny. Did she ever say anything about her or her friends turning tricks for McNally?"

"Right, Pete. She told me that she was fucking strangers for money in a farm house. Is that what you think? That she would tell me that? Get real, will you?"

Drollstrom glared at him. "Just why did you break up with her? Tell me again, Ronny. I forget."

Ronny's face turned red, as he tried to hold back his anger. "You dammed well know why."

"That's right. She cheated on you, didn't she? Do you think that was the only guy she cheated with? I bet there were hundreds."

"Shut the fuck up, Pete," Ott said.

"Or what?" Drollstrom whispered. "Whatcha gonna do, Ott? Hit me here in front of everyone? You gonna hit a cop?" he said, a smug look on his face.

Ronny clenched his fists, fighting to control his temper. He stood up, threw a sawbuck on the table, and turned to leave. He stopped, turned back, and looked at Drollstrom. "You damned right I am," he said, as he brought his arm back, followed through, and hit Drollstrom square in the chin, knocking him off of his chair onto the dirty floor.

Ronny looked over at the three men who were sitting at the bar. One of them gave him the thumbs up and smiled. "Didn't see a thing," he told Ronny, smiling, and turned back to his drink.

Ronny glanced down at Drollstrom, turned, and

walked towards the door.

"I'm gonna fucking kill you," Drollstrom shouted. "You hear me, Ott? I'm gonna fucking kill you for this."

Two hours later, half the town knew that Officer Peter Drollstrom had had his ass kicked by Ronny Ott in Fireman's Tavern. Chief Austin heard about it from Jacquie, who heard about it from her boyfriend, who was a friend of Ronny.

"About time somebody laid his ass out," he muttered. "I'm surprised it doesn't happen more often."

Jacquie grinned. "From what I heard, he threatened to kill Ronny. Do you think we should keep an eye on him?"

Austin laughed. "I don't think that's necessary. When the day comes that Drollstrom has enough guts to kill someone, I'll quit this job and retire."

"Stranger things have happened," Jacquie commented. "What's going on with Debbie Nelson's case? Anything new?"

"Not a thing. I have a feeling that we're never going to find out what happened."

"Do you think you should call in some outside help?"

"I thought about it, but I can't see what they are going to find that I didn't. Either nobody knows anything or they aren't talking. I'm at a dead-end here, Jacquie, and it's keeping me awake nights thinking about it."

"Well, at least it's been quiet for the past few days."

"You know what they say, don't you?"

"That it's always the quietest before the storm?" Jacquie replied.

"Nope. I was thinking more along the lines of 'things never get so bad that they can't get worse'."

"Same difference," she said.

Austin sat back in his chair and looked up at the ceiling. "This place could use some new paint," he stated.

"I guess," Jacquie agreed.

"It's Tommy's birthday today," Austin told her.

"Really? How old is he?"

"Eleven."

"Eleven already? Boy, times sure flies by, doesn't it?"

"Seems like every year goes a little faster," Austin commented.

"Is he having a party?"

"It's just the family tonight. I guess Catherine has a bowling party planned for Saturday."

"That should be fun."

"I guess." Austin glanced up at the clock on the wall and sighed. "It's almost six. I guess I'll head on home."

"Have a good night, then," Jacquie told him. "I'll see you tomorrow."

Austin picked up his hat, put it on, and walked towards the door. "Night, Jacquie."

"Good night, Augie. See you tomorrow. And, wish Tommy a happy birthday for me, will you?"

116

Chapter Twenty-two

The fire siren went off at 11:10 p.m. Twelve firemen grabbed their gear, hurried out of their homes, and headed for the fire station. Four more volunteers, who had just finished bowling their third and last game at the bowling alley, downed their beers and ran out of the building to join their fellow firefighters.

The wailing of the siren woke Chief Austin. A few seconds later he received a phone call informing him that there was a fire at the old McNally farm. He was dressed and on his way to the scene of the fire in less than five minutes.

Austin pulled in behind the fire truck, got out of his car, and looked over at the blazing inferno. He immediately knew that there was no way this house could be saved. The best the firemen could do would be to keep it from spreading to the out buildings.

"It's no use. Let it burn," he heard one of the firemen shout to the man next to him. "It's gone."

Austin watched the activity for a few more minutes and, knowing that there was nothing he could do, decided to go back home. Officer Benisch was there and had everything under control. He got in his car and headed back towards Columbus. Fifteen minutes later, he had crawled back into his bed, was asleep, and snoring.

At four o'clock a.m. Austin's phone rang again. He reached over, grabbed the handpiece, and answered the call. "Austin."

He listened to the caller on the other end of the line. He sat up and threw his legs over the side of the bed. "Do you know who it is, Benny?"

His wife, Catherine, rolled over and opened her eyes. "What is it?" she uttered.

Austin motioned for her to be quiet. "Are you sure?" he asked Officer Benisch.

"Thanks. I'll be there shortly," he said and hung up the phone.

"What's wrong?" Catherine asked him.

"They found a body."

"Who did, dear?"

Austin turned and looked at her. "I'm sorry I woke you. Go back to sleep."

"Augie," Catherine said, "tell me what's going on. It's four o'clock in the morning."

"There was a fire tonight."

"I know, dear. I heard the siren. Where was it?"

"It was that old house out on the McNally farm. It's totally gone. They couldn't save it."

"That's a real shame. How come Benny called? Is there a problem?"

"It seems that when the firemen were shifting through the debris, they found a body. They think it's a man, but they're not sure."

"Oh, my goodness. That's awful."

"It is," Austin agreed, as he finished dressing.

Catherine was quiet for a few moments. "Augie," she said, "I thought that house was empty."

"As far as I know, no one has lived there since old man McNally died. I've got to get out there,

118

Catherine. We'll talk later." He bent down and kissed her forehead. "Try to get back to sleep."

"Do you have any idea who it might be?" Fire Chief Robert Williams asked Austin.

Austin shook his head no. "There's no way in hell anyone could identify him. If it even is a him. The body is burned way beyond recognition, Bob."

"I know. Do you figure it might be some transit that broke in to spend the night? Fell asleep smoking or something?"

Austin shrugged. "Could be. I doubt it's anyone from around here. Damned shame, whoever it is."

"What should we do with the body?" Williams inquired.

"Let's wait a few hours and then call Jones' Funeral Home. No need to wake them up this early. I'll have them store it until the medical examiner can pick it up.

"You gonna call them?" Williams asked.

"I guess I can do that. You want to go get some coffee?"

Williams gave him a questioning look. "What's open at this time or the day?"

"Right. I forgot it's so early. I guess I'll head over to the station. No sense in going back home now."

"Shitty way to start the day," Williams declared.

"You got that right." Austin looked down at the body and sighed. "I wonder if we'll ever find out who that is."

"You stupid son of a bitch," McNally yelled into

the phone. "There was somebody in the house. What the hell is wrong with you? Jesus, I can't believe you're so stupid."

Drollstrom rubbed his eyes and looked at the clock radio next to his bed. "It's only six-thirty. How the hell do you know that already?" he asked.

"Everybody in town who's awake knows there was a body in that house when it burned down. What the fuck did you do, Pete?"

"What the hell are you so mad for? I did what you asked. I burned your fucking house down."

"Did it ever occur to you to wait until the house was empty?"

"You said to burn it down last night. That's exactly what I did."

"I didn't tell you to burn some poor bum along with it," Pat shouted. "Fuck! Please, tell me it was a bum and not somebody from here."

"It was just a bum. I didn't know he was there. I looked up and there he was, watching me through a window. He saw me pouring gasoline around the house. I couldn't have a witness to what I was doing, for fuck's sake. I had to get rid of him."

McNally suddenly felt sick to his stomach. "Did you kill him before you set the house on fire?"

"Of course not. I only knocked him out. I hit him over the head with my tire iron."

"Good God in heaven. You fucking burned him alive, Pete!"

"He was a fucking bum. Nobody's gonna miss him."

"If anyone finds out about this. . ."

"Nobody's gonna find out. And, this makes us even, McNally. I'm not doing any more of your dirty work. Got it?"

"Oh, I've got it all right. Asking you to do this was the biggest mistake I've ever made. Believe me, it won't happen again.

"I want my bullet," Drollstrom said.

McNally didn't say anything.

"Did you hear me, Pat? I want that fucking bullet back."

"I hear you. But you know what I think I'll do with that bullet? I think I'm going to put it in a safe place, along with a note explaining how I got it. If anything happens to me – well, your ass is grass."

"You son of a bitch."

"I guess that makes two of us, Pete. But at least I haven't murdered anyone," he lied.

Chapter Twenty-three

"You look like shit," Dr. Jerry Severson stated.

"Thanks. It's always nice to hear that. I'm running a little low on gas right now, Jerry. It's been a rough twelve hours."

"I'd say you're having a rough week. You've had a couple of murders, a suspicious fire, and a cooked body that you can't identify. And, the week isn't even over."

"Georgie," Austin called to the young woman behind the counter. "More coffee, please," he said, holding up his cup.

"I'm not sure about the fire being suspicious," Austin told Severson. "I figure it was just some bum that fell asleep while smoking. An insurance investigator will probably be called in to check it out, though."

"Pat McNally owns that place, doesn't he?"

"He does. His grandpa willed it to him. It would have gone to Paddy, Pat's father, but he died a few months before the old man. It was pretty hard on Pat, losing his dad and grandpa within a few months of each other."

"Does the kid live here in Columbus?"

"He has a house up by the hospital on Charles St. Nice place. I figure he's worth a few bucks, mostly from what he's inherited. If he has a job, I sure don't know what it is."

"Must be nice not having to work."

"I'd say so. He shot himself in the leg the other night. He says it happened while he was cleaning his gun."

"You don't believe him?" Severson inquired.

"I'm not sure if I do or not. He's been around guns all his life and it doesn't make sense that he'd be that careless, that's all. Plus, he got the doctor to give him the bullet, which he says he lost, so I can't check out his story."

"Well, you've got enough on your plate without adding him to the mix."

"Guess you're right about that."

Severson pushed his plate away from him and wiped his mouth with a napkin. "That hit the spot. I guess I better go pick up that body and get back to work. Call me if you need anything."

"Do you think the teeth will be of any use?" Austin asked as he lit up a cigarette.

"I doubt it," Severson answered. He scooted out of the booth and stood up, ready to leave. "I doubt our mystery man ever saw a dentist."

"You're sure it was a man?"

"No, but the odds are that it is. Anyway, thanks for breakfast. See you."

Austin glanced up at him. "I gather I'm buying."

"You gather correctly."

"Where have you been?" Jacquie asked Austin, as he walked into the police station. "It's after ten."

"I was having breakfast with Jerry Severson. Are you keeping tabs on me now, Jacquie?"

Jacquie grinned. "That's what Catherine pays me for."

"Has Drollstrom shown up for work yet?"

"He has. He was here before eight, all excited to hear about the big fire last night."

"Whatcha tell him?"

"Not much to tell. There was a fire. McNally's farm house burned down. A man was found dead inside." She hesitated for a few seconds. "I wonder if that man was dead before the fire started or if the fire killed him. What do you think?"

Austin thought for a few moments. "You bring up a good point. Doc Severson will check that out."

"He'll be able to tell if he died from smoke inhalation, won't he?" Jacquie asked.

"I think he will if there are enough of his lungs left to examine. I'm surprised he could even tell it was a man. He'll be sending me his final report in a day or two. I'll know then."

"Ronny Ott called a little while ago. He wouldn't tell me what he wanted. He just asked if you were here and when I said you were out, he hung up."

"I wonder what that's all about."

"I figure he'll call back if it's important," Jacquie said.

"I need to see you."

"Pat, do you know what time it is?"

"Of course, I do."

"I just left your place a few hours ago. What do you want now?

"I think I'm going to have to kill Drollstrom. He's a walking time bomb. Plus, I think he told somebody I asked him to burn my house down."

Sandra reached for a pack of cigarettes on the

nightstand, shook one loose, and lit it. "You're paranoid," she told him, as she blew out the smoke.

"I'm telling you, I can't trust him."

"Don't you think you should have thought about that before you got him involved with all this shit? Hell, Pat, I would have burned that place down for you if you had asked me. But, nooo, you had to ask that idiot to do it."

"What do you think I should do?"

Sandra laughed. "Well, for starters, I don't think you should kill him."

"I'm serious," Pat exclaimed. "This isn't funny."

"I know," Sandra said. "He really did fuck up, didn't he? Now, that place will be crawling with the cops and insurance investigators and god only knows who else. You don't think they'll look down the well, do you?"

"Ah, shit, Sandra! Did you have to bring that up? That's just something else I have to worry about now. Shit, anyway."

"Will you relax? There's no reason anyone is going to look down the well. I was just kidding."

"Again – not funny."

"What are you going to do the rest of the day?"

"Do you really care?"

"Of course, I do," Sandra told him.

"I'm gonna watch some television while I watch my leg heal."

"I'll bring you lunch," Sandra said.

"Will you pick up a couple of six-packs, too? I'm out of beer."

"Will do. By the way, Pat. . ." she hesitated.

"What?"

"I was just wondering. Do you have any idea when you'll get the insurance money?"

Pat laughed. "You never disappoint."

Chapter Twenty-four

"Who was that?" Austin inquired, as Jacquie hung up the phone.

"Donald Vinz, from Jones' Funeral Home. He wanted to know if we're all set for Arlis Upton's funeral this afternoon."

"What did you tell him?"

"That we're good to go. I thought you were listening," she said.

"With one ear, maybe. I was thinking about Debbie and the fact that I haven't gotten any closer to finding out what happened to her than I was on Sunday. I think I'm gonna talk to her friends again."

"What good will that do? They aren't gonna tell you anything."

Austin walked over to the window and looked outside. "Are you going to Arlis' funeral?" he asked.

"Boy, you are distracted, aren't you," Jacquie said. "I'm the lead car to the cemetery. You know that."

"Right," Austin said, half paying attention. He turned and walked back to his desk. "Who do you think is most likely to talk?" he asked Jacquie.

"You mean of the four of them?"

"Ya. Who do you think is most likely to cave under some pressure?"

"Well, definitely not Sandra. You could push bamboo sticks under her fingernails and she wouldn't talk. Annie is almost as tough, but she'll do whatever Sandra tells her to. Karen is the quiet one. You never quite know what she's thinking. But I think she's a follower and just goes along with whatever. You probably would get the most out of Rose, as long as you separate her from the pack. I think she's the one who would spill the beans, if there are any beans to be spilled."

"Oh, there are plenty of beans, believe me. Those four have been holding back since Debbie was killed. I can feel it."

"Well, then, Rose would be the one you need to talk to first," Jacquie remarked.

"Do you think she's home right now?" Austin asked.

"Probably. I'm beginning to wonder if she even has a job."

"Call her," Austin suddenly blurted out.

"What?"

"Call her and tell her I want her down here in thirty minutes."

"And, the reason she is being summoned, if she asks, is what?"

"I don't know, Jacquie. Make something up. Just get her down here. I want to talk to her before we have to leave for Arlis' funeral."

"All right. I'll call her. But I can't guarantee anything," Jacquie said, picking up the phone.

Rose hung up the phone. She wasn't sure if she had to go talk to Chief Austin or not. Jacquie had been polite and friendly when she asked her to come into the station. She had agreed, but now she was having second thoughts about talking to Austin.

She picked up the phone and dialed Sandra's number, figuring that she would know if she had to talk to Austin or not. She waited but there was no answer. As she hung up the phone, she realized that her hands were shaking. Trying to hold it together, she glanced around the room, hoping the answer would suddenly appear. Maybe Sandra's at Pat's, she thought and dialed his number.

She held her breath, waiting. Finally, after the fifth ring, Pat answered the call.

"Pat," she said, starting to cry, "Austin wants to see me down at the station. I don't know. . ."

"Rose, are you okay? You're mumbling."

"I need Sandra. Is she there?"

"No, she's not. What's the matter? Why are you crying?"

"I'm scared, that's why. Jacquie Gorski called me and told me that Chief Austin wants to see me. He wants me to go to the police station, so he can talk to me. I don't know what to do, Pat. What should I do?" she asked, still crying, making it difficult for Pat to understand her.

"When did she call you?" Pat asked.

"Just now. Do I have to go talk to him?"

Pat sat back in his chair and thought about Rose's question. "Damn," he muttered to himself.

"What did you say?" Rose asked. "I couldn't hear you."

"Did Jacquie give you any idea why he wants to see you or what he wants to talk about?"

"No. She just said I should be there in thirty minutes."

"Don't go," Pat told her. "You don't have to go."

"Are you sure? Won't I be in trouble if I don't

129

go?"

"You don't have to talk to him, Rose. He can't make you. Where are Karen and Annie?"

"They went shopping in Madison."

"So, you're alone there in your apartment?"

"Yes."

"Stay there for now. Don't answer the door or the phone. If I call, I'll let it ring twice, hang up, and call you back. Got it?"

"What if Austin comes over here?" Rose said, nervously.

"I just told you, don't answer the door," Pat said, raising his voice.

"I'm sorry, Pat. Don't be mad. I'm scared, that's all."

"I'm sorry, Rose. I shouldn't have yelled at you. I know you're worried."

Rose smiled, pleased that Pat wasn't upset with her after all. "If you see Sandra, would you ask her to come over?" she asked him

"Actually, Rose, I was planning on having a little meeting with all of you tonight. There are a few things we need to go over. I was thinking round eight would be good."

"Should I tell the others?" Rose asked.

"No. I'll let them know. . ." He hesitated. "You know what, Rose? I have a better idea. Why don't you come over now so you and I can have some alone time before the others get here? How does that sound?"

"I'll be right there. Thank you, Pat. I was so nervous about talking to Chief Austin."

"Don't you worry about a thing. I'll see you in a

few."

Rose hesitated a moment. "Is there anything special you want me to wear?" she asked him, giggling.

Pat laughed. "I know what I don't want you to wear, Rose?"

"What's that?" she said softly.

"Leave your panties at home tonight. It will be our little secret."

Rose giggled. "You're so bad. See ya," she said and hung up.

Chapter Twenty-five

Chief Austin glanced up at the clock. "She's not coming," he commented. "It's been over an hour, and we need to go. Arlis' funeral is about to start."

"I don't understand it," Jacquie said. "When I talked to Rose, she said she'd be right over."

"Somebody got to her."

"Maybe. Anyway, she's not going anywhere. I'll call her after the funeral is over."

"You look nice in your dress blues," Austin told Jacquie."

"Thanks. You clean up pretty good, too." She adjusted her cap. "Is it straight?" she asked Austin.

"It's fine," he told her. "I hate this, Jacquie. We aren't supposed to bury our children. It isn't supposed to work that way."

"I know," Jacquie replied. "And, the thing that really stinks is that we have to do this all over again tomorrow."

"We'll need the entire force working tomorrow. I figure half the town will show up for Debbie's funeral."

"They should have done private," Jacquie said. "It's gonna be a friggin' circus."

"I'm afraid you're right."

"Did you get in touch with Kirk Peary?"

"I did and he said he'd take pictures. I asked him to be available today and tomorrow. It's a long shot. I doubt the pictures will help us, but you just never know."

"Ready?"

Austin grabbed his hat from off of his desk.

"Let's go."

Four hours later, Chief Austin, Deputy Gorski, Officer Benisch, and Officer Leyson were back at the police station.

"I thought there would be more people there," Leyson commented.

"Me, too," Benisch said. "You know who was missing, don't you?"

"Of course, I do," Austin said, angrily. "It doesn't speak well of him and it reflects poorly on us. What could Sam have been thinking, not to show up for his girlfriend's funeral?"

"When was the last time you talked to him?" Leyson asked.

"A few days ago. I told him to take some time off. You know, to work through what happened to Arlis. But I certainly didn't expect that he wouldn't show up for her funeral."

"Do you think I should call him? You know, to find out if he's okay," Jacquie asked.

"Where's Drollstrom?" Austin suddenly asked, changing the subject.

"He's out on patrol," Jacquie said. "Why?"

"Call him on the radio. I want to know where he is."

Just as Jacquie reached for the mike, Drollstrom yelled over the speaker, "Chief, are you there? Chief? Over!"

Austin grabbed the mike, "Austin, here. Over."

"I'm up at the cemetery, Chief. You better get up here. Over."

133

"What's up, Pete? Over."

"It's Sam. He's dead, Augie. Over."

"Say again. Over."

"Sam's dead. I found him in his car. Over."

"Where exactly are you? Over."

"I'm at the far end of the Catholic cemetery. Over."

"Don't touch anything. I'm on my way. Over and out."

"Chief?" Jacquie whispered, tears rolling down her cheeks. "Not Sam. Please tell me Pete didn't just say that Sam is dead."

"Not now, Jacquie. Now is not the time to fall apart. We've got a job to do. Let's go," he said, heading for the door.

"Chief, could we say a prayer first?" Benisch asked.

Austin stared at him, surprised at his request. He took a step back and bowed his head. "Make it short."

Officer Sam Lober was in the driver's seat; his body slumped forward over the steering wheel. The first thing that Austin noticed was that the back of Sam's head was gone. The second thing he took note of was that Sam's revolver was lying on the seat next to him. "Shit!" he said, barely loud enough for anyone to hear.

"He ate his gun," Jacquie whispered. "This is going to kill his folks."

"Keep everyone back," Austin instructed. He turned and looked at Officer Benisch. "Benny, go back to the station and call Severson. Tell him we need him here as soon as possible."

"There's an envelope on the dash," Jacquie said, gloving up.

"Leave it," Austin said.

She pulled her hand back and looked at him. "It's probably a suicide note."

"It can wait a few minutes," Austin told her and walked away from the car towards a big oak tree.

"Where are you going?" Jacquie yelled, starting to follow him.

Austin waved her off, walked behind the tree, and vomited. He straightened up and looked out over the countryside, taking in deep breaths, trying to clear his head. It wasn't until he wiped his face with the back of his hand that he realized he was crying.

"Did he admit to killing Arlis?" Severson asked Austin.

Austin poured another shot of Jack into his glass and took a sip. "Nope." He reached into the top drawer of his desk and took out an envelope and handed it to the doctor. "Read it for yourself."

Austin took another sip of his drink, watching Severson's face as he read the note. Severson looked at him and shook his head. "It doesn't say much."

"No, it doesn't. He says that he loves his parents and he's sorry. He said he loved Arlis and can't go on without her and he can't live in a town where people think he killed her. That's it." Austin stared up at the ceiling. "I failed him, Jerry. I didn't catch the monster who killed her and Sam couldn't live with it."

Severson held his glass out, indicating that Austin should pour him another drink. "Make it a short one. I've got to get going," he told Austin.

"It's been one fucking rotten day," Austin declared. "If I had to guess, I'd say one of the worst I've ever had."

"What was Drollstrom doing up at the cemetery?" Severson asked.

"What?" Austin asked, surprised at the question.

"Well, there's not a hell of a lot of traffic out that way, so I doubt he was watching for speeders. I was just wondering what he was doing there."

Austin sat back and stared at him. "That's a hell of a good question."

Chapter Twenty-six

Sandra jumped out of her car and ran into the house, slamming the front door behind her.

"Leave the door open, will you? It's hot in here."

"What the fuck did you do, Pat?" she yelled.

Pat looked away, not able to look her in the eyes.

"Where is she?"

"In the bedroom."

Sandra turned and walked down the short hallway to Pat's bedroom and looked into the room. Rose was laid out on the bed, her hands resting on her chest. She looks like she's sleeping, Sandra thought. She stood in the doorway, hesitant to enter. Finally, she walked over to the bed and felt Rose's neck, checking to see if she had a pulse.

"Pat," she shouted, "get your ass in here."

"Seriously, I thought she was dead," Pat said. "We got into this big fight and she locked herself in the bathroom. When she didn't come out, I forced the door open and found her on the floor along with that pill bottle lying next to her."

Sandra reached down and smoothed Rose's hair away from her face. "And, you thought she was dead," Sandra declared.

"Look at her," Pat cried out, "does she look like she's alive to you?"

Sandra looked down at the sleeping woman and smiled. "She does look like she's dead, doesn't she? Well, lucky for you, she's not. We need to get a shitload of coffee in her and get her walking."

"Do you think she'll be okay?" Pat asked.

Sandra looked at him and shrugged. "She probably will be, but what do I know? She's done this before, you know."

Pat looked surprised. "I didn't know that."

"It's her way of getting attention. I'm afraid that one of these days she's gonna take it too far and really kill herself. Go make some coffee, will you?"

Ten minutes later, when Pat walked into his bedroom, Sandra had Rose sitting on the edge of the bed. Sandra looked up at Pat. "Would you care to tell me why Rose hasn't got any panties on?" she asked, angrily.

"She arrived that way," Pat said, turning a little red in the face.

"Really? And, what was she doing here, anyway, Pat?"

"Let's get her up and walking. Why don't you grab that side? I'll explain everything to you in a minute." Pat reached down and helped Sandra pull Rose to her feet. "Let's go," he said.

"No!" Rose yelled and pushed the coffee cup away from her mouth. "I've had enough of that swill."

Sandra set the cup on the coffee table and glanced over at Pat. "You okay," she asked him.

"I will be. I'm sorry I wasn't more help. It's hard to walk without my cane."

Sandra sat down next to him on the couch. She stared at Rose, who was curled up on the overstuffed chair, softly crying. "So, everything that you just told me is true?" Sandra asked him.

"Of course," Pat replied. "I sure as hell didn't make it up. She was a basket case. If Austin had talked to her when she was in that frame of mind, she would have told him everything. I needed her where I could keep an eye on her."

"Which would be here?"

"Of course. I couldn't go to her place, with my leg and all, so I told her to come here."

"Without any panties?" Sandra inquired, grinning.

"That was a joke. I didn't think she'd actually show up without any underwear. That's why she got so upset. She thought we were going to have sex and when I told her that wasn't going to happen, she lost it."

"Why didn't you just fuck her?"

Pat sat back and stared at her. "Seriously, Sandra? Out of all the women in this town, she's the last one I want to fuck."

Sandra laughed. "Me, too."

"What are we gonna do with her?" Pat asked, grinning at her last remark.

Sandra shrugged. "I don't know. Eventually, Austin is going to talk to her and I don't think she'll keep quiet. We've got an awful lot to lose if she starts talking."

Pat looked at Rose and frowned. "You know what we need to do, don't you?"

"It has to look like an accident," Sandra said.

"What does?" Pat asked.

"Her death. Why, what were you talking about?"

Pat looked shocked. "You want to kill her? Holy shit, Sandra. I meant we had to get her to leave town for a while. Not kill her."

Sandra didn't say anything, thinking about the situation. "If she leaves town, she'll eventually come back. And, there's no way she'll be able to make it on her own. If she leaves forever, we don't have to worry about her talking. I don't think we'll ever be able to trust her, Pat. And. . . Well, I know this sounds bad, but with her out of the picture, that's one less partner and more money for the rest of us."

"You're joking, right?" Pat asked her.

"About the money?"

"No, not the money. About killing her."

"Were there any pills left in that bottle?"

"Come on, Sandra. You can't be serious. This is Rose we're talking about."

"Oh, I'm serious, all right. Where are the pills?"

Pat reached into his pocket and pulled out a small bottle and handed them to her. "You better think long and hard before you do anything. This is serious shit."

Sandra leaned over and kissed him on the cheek. "I hate it when you get so serious. Smile, will you?"

"I don't feel good," Rose mumbled. "I think I'm gonna be sick."

"I need to get her home," Sandra told Pat. She removed the top of the pill bottle and looked inside. "I think there are enough pills left to do the trick,"

"Be sure to wipe our prints off of that bottle," Pat instructed her.

"Rose, honey," Sandra said. "I'm gonna take you home now, so you can get some rest. Do you think you can make it to the car on your own?"

"I guess. I'm really tired, Sandra."

"I know you are. As soon as we get to your place, I'll give you something to help you sleep. Okay?"

"Okay. Thanks, Sandra."

Sandra reached down, helped Rose out of the chair, and started towards the door. She turned to Pat. "Call them now, Pat. I want them out of there before I get Rose home."

"Are you coming? Rose mumbled.

"I'll be right there. You go get in the car," Sandra told her. "Pat?"

"I'm on it. Are you sure this is the only way to handle this, Sandra?"

"Will you just fucking call them? And, please be sure that you don't tell them that Rose was here. Okay, Pat?"

Pat shot a dirty look at her. "Give me a little credit, will you?" he said, as he reached for the phone.

Sandra stood in the doorway and watched him dial the number.

"Annie? Good, you're home. Are Karen and Rose with you? I need to talk to you, like right now. Can you guys come over?"

Pat listened for a moment. "Rose isn't there? Do you know where she is?"

He gave Sandra the thumbs up while listening to Annie. "Yes, Sandra's coming, too. I just called her," he replied.

"All right. I'll see you in a few minutes. Bye."

Pat looked at Sandra and frowned. "This isn't right, Sandra."

"Are you willing to risk it? She'll talk, you know."

"I know. Just be careful."

"Oh, fuck!" Sandra exclaimed.

"What now?"

"Rose's car. It's out front. Shit, Pat, we've got one too many cars here."

Pat thought for a minute. "My car's in the garage. I'll hide Rose's car in there and park mine in the driveway. You take Rose home in your car. You have to be driving your car when you come back here."

"But Rose's car needs to be at her place. If it's not there when they find her. . ." Sandra said, raising her voice.

"Calm down," Pat told her, interrupting her. "It will be there."

"How are you. . .?"

"Sandra, you need to leave. Now!"

Chapter Twenty-seven

"We need to move out," Chief Austin told his fellow officers. "The Nelson funeral is in forty-five minutes. Are there any questions?"

The room was silent.

"Pete, you have the lead car today. Try to keep it under twenty, will you? Jacquie, you take the 4 corners and, Benny, I want you at the intersection of James and Lewis St. That leaves you, Matt. I want you stationed at the entrance to the cemetery. Everyone got that?"

"I have a question, Chief," Drollstrom said.

"What's that, Pete?"

"What am I supposed to drive? My squad car is in the shop being repaired."

Chief Austin glared at him. "I hope you're not serious. Your vehicle is scheduled to be repaired next week, so why is it there now?"

"George called and said they had an earlier opening, so I took the car over there last night and dropped it off."

Austin looked at Jacquie, who had just sat down at her desk. "Jacquie, call. . ."

"I'm on it," Jacquie interrupted, reaching for the phone.

"You had better hope that they haven't started working on it yet, Pete, or I'll make you lead that fucking funeral procession to the cemetery on roller skates," Austin yelled.

"What's the big deal, anyway?" he yelled back. "I'll use the other squad."

"Change of plans," Austin said. "Benny, you're the lead car. Matt, you take the intersection at James and Lewis."

"What about me?" Drollstrom asked.

"Is everyone clear on your positions?" Austin asked, ignoring Drollstrom.

Drollstrom looked around the room, hoping to find some support. "What about me?" he asked again, realizing that no one was going to help him out.

"You are assigned the entrance to the cemetery, Officer Drollstrom. I'm going to drive you up there and drop you off. You will stand, at attention, by the entrance until the last car of the procession has entered the cemetery. Understood?"

"But, that's gonna be hours from now and it's hot out. You don't expect me to stand and wait up there until the funeral is over, do you? At least, let me take my car so I have a place to sit until everyone gets there."

"No."

"But, Augie. . ."

"Chief Austin! Show me some respect and don't call me Augie. Understand!" Austin shouted. He closed his eyes and took a deep breath, trying to keep control of his temper.

"Chief?" Jacquie said as she hung up the phone.

"What is it?"

"They've already started working on the car."

"It doesn't make any difference now, Jacquie." Austin poured himself a cup of coffee, walked over to his desk, and sat. "It's time for you to get going," he said.

He watched as his officers gathered up their gear and started to walk out. Drollstrom looked at Austin, not sure what he was supposed to do.

"Aren't we leaving?" Drollstrom asked.

"In a minute. I'm just going to sit back and enjoy this fine cup of coffee first," Austin said softly.

Drollstrom walked over to his desk and sat down, waiting for Austin to make the next move.

"My dad's gonna hear about this, you know," Pete said.

"I think it's best if you kept quiet right now, Pete," Austin said softly.

Austin threw the shovel to the ground, reached into his back pocket, and pulled out a hanky. He looked down at the ground as he wiped the sweat from his forehead, satisfied that there was no way Drollstrom could remove himself from the deep hole.

"How you doing down there," he said, looking at Drollstrom's head, which was the only part of his body that was not covered in sand.

"My father will kill you for this," Drollstrom screamed. "Let me out of this hole, you bastard."

"Your daddy isn't going to bail you out of this one, Petey," Austin said and started to walk away.

"Where are you going?" Drollstrom yelled. "Come back here."

Austin turned back towards him and smiled. "Don't get so excited. I'll be right back."

Drollstrom watched as Austin walked to his car and opened the truck. He reached inside and took out a bag, shut the trunk, and walked back to where

Drollstrom was buried.

"See, I said I'd be right back."

Austin reached inside the bag, took out a jar of honey, and opened it.

"What is that? What are you doing?" Drollstrom shouted.

"Well, how lucky am I?" Austin said, as he tipped the jar and watched the honey pour out onto Drollstrom's head. "This honey is really runny. I guess the heat softened it up a lot."

"Stop!" Drollstrom screamed. "For god's sake, let me out of here."

"Sorry. No can do." Austin told him, as he threw the empty jar onto the ground, walked back to his car, and got in behind the steering wheel.

"Come back," Drollstrom screamed.

"Don't let the ants get in your pants," Austin yelled, as he drove away, smiling.

Austin finished his coffee and set the cup down on his desk. He looked over at Drollstrom and realized that Drollstrom was staring at him. He grinned, stood up, and grabbed his hat.

"What's so fucking funny?" Drollstrom asked.

"Let's go, Pete," he said, as the phone on his desk rang.

"You gonna answer that?"

Austin hesitated, then reached down and picked up the phone. "Columbus Police Department, Austin here."

Drollstrom watched the expression change on Austin's face and immediately knew it was bad news.

"Is she alive?" Austin asked.

Drollstrom waited, wondering who Austin was referring to.

"I have the Nelson funeral, but I'll be in after that," Austin told the person on the other end of the call and hung up the phone.

Chapter Twenty-eight

"She's brain dead," Dr. Poszert said factually. "Her brain was deprived of oxygen for too long. It's unfortunate that the emergency room doctor brought her back. She would have been better off if he hadn't resuscitated her."

Chief Austin looked over at Rose. "So, it's the machines keeping her alive?"

"Basically, they are, for now. There's a possibility that she may breathe on her own again, but between us, Augie, I doubt it."

"When was she admitted?"

Dr. Poszert looked down at the clip board he was holding and checked the attached medical form. "It looks like emergency got the call around eight-thirty this morning."

Austin was quiet for a few moments. "Does it say who called it in?" he asked.

Dr. Poszert shook his head no. "That information isn't on the form, but, if I remember correctly, she lives with a couple of roommates. I imagine it was one of them that found her and called for help."

"Annie Berg and Karen Berke."

"Right," Dr. Poszert. "Nice young women. They're patients of mine."

Chief Austin smiled. "Isn't everyone, Doc?"

"Not quite. There are other doctors in this town, you know."

"What did the blood tests show? Some kind of overdose, I imagine."

"Sleeping pills. They found an empty bottle in

her bedroom. Although, I don't think the bottle was full when she took the pills. If it had been, she would be dead right now."

"Did you write the prescription?"

"No, it wasn't me. They were prescribed by a doctor in Sun Prairie," Dr. Poszert told him.

"Name?"

"A Dr. Derr. And, I don't know the man so I can't tell you anything about him."

"I'll check him out. I've got to get going. Let me know if her condition changes, will you?"

"Of course."

"Thanks."

"How is she?" Jacquie asked, as soon as Austin walked into the police station.

"Not good. Doc Poszert said it would be a blessing if she doesn't make it. She's brain dead, which means she'll probably be in a vegetative state for the rest of her life."

"Some people come back," Jacquie said.

"Sometimes I hate this job," Austin uttered.

"I know. Me, too," Jacquie said. "But then we save someone and it makes it all worthwhile. You just have to learn to take the bad with the good, I guess. Anyway, let's hope she comes out of it and makes a full recovery."

"That's all we can do." Austin pulled a cigarette out of the pack and looked at it. "I've got to cut back on these damned things," he declared. "It's getting too expensive. They're up to a quarter a pack and God only knows how much they'll cost next year. It's ridiculous."

"You're right," Jacquie agreed. "It seems just like yesterday we were only paying fifteen cents a pack."

Austin lit the cigarette and exhaled the smoke. "I'm going to go talk to Annie and Karen. I'd like you to come with."

"Are you leaving right now?"

"In a few minutes. Will you get a hold of Pete and tell him I want him to come in and man the office while we're gone?"

"I wouldn't be surprised if he's parked somewhere taking a nap," Jacquie commented, grinning. "He really got a bad sunburn on his face this morning."

"It wouldn't have been so bad if he had put his hat on while he was waiting."

Karen and Annie were both crying, making it hard for Austin to understand anything they were saying. He sat back in his chair and looked over at Jacquie, who looked back at him and shrugged.

He waited until Annie got her crying under control before he spoke again. "Let's start over, shall we?" he asked the two women. "Annie, you found her, right?"

Annie shook her head up and down.

"Do you remember what time it was?"

"Around eight-thirty," she said. "We had to get ready for Debbie's funeral and she wasn't up yet, so I went in to wake her and found her. . ." She took a deep breath, as she started to tear up again. "I'm sorry," she told Austin.

"Just take your time, Annie. It was around eight-thirty. What did you do then?"

"I knew something was wrong. I shook her but she wouldn't wake up. Karen called for help and we just waited. There was nothing we could do. She wouldn't wake up," Annie exclaimed, raising her voice.

"Did you see her last night?" Austin asked.

Annie looked up at him, a confused look on her face. "Last night? Why do you need to know that?"

"Were you with Rose last night, Annie?" Austin asked again.

"No. We don't know where she was, do we, Karen?"

Karen reached over and pulled a tissue out of its box and blew her nose. "No. We went shopping in Madison yesterday. Rose didn't want to go. We didn't see her after that."

"So, the last time you saw her was yesterday morning?"

"That's right," Annie replied.

"Were you here all night?"

"No," Annie told him. "Karen and I went out. We would have asked Rose to come with us, but she wasn't here. Like I said, I don't know where she was or what she did yesterday."

"What time did you get home last night?" Austin asked.

Annie thought for a moment. "I guess it was around twelve-thirty or one o'clock. Right, Karen?"

Karen shook her head. "That sounds about right."

"And, Rose wasn't here when you came home?"

"I don't think so but, I . . .." She glanced over at Karen. "I never checked her room," she said. "Did you, Karen?"

"No. I went straight to bed."

"Then, she could have been here?" Austin inquired.

"I guess," Annie said. "Oh, my god," she cried out. "Karen, she might have been here. If we had checked her room, we might have seen that something was wrong." She stared at Austin. "We might have saved her," she said, starting to cry again.

"You don't know that," Jacquie said. "You don't know if she was here or not. You can't start blaming yourselves for what happened."

"Karen," Austin said, "can you think of any reason why Rose would try to kill herself?"

Karen sat back and shook her head no. "Of course not. You don't even know for sure if she did try to kill herself. For all we know, it was an accident. And, unless someone can prove to me otherwise, that's what I'm calling it. An accident!"

Austin glanced over at Jacquie, looking for her reaction to the outburst. Jacquie's expression didn't change. "How about you, Annie?" she said.

"What?" Annie asked, sounding a little defensive.

"Can you think of a reason?"

"It was an accident," Karen yelled. "That's all there is to it. Why don't you stop looking for things that aren't there, for god's sake? Go find the person who killed Debbie. And, Arlis. Do you even have a clue who killed them? Why don't you spend your time doing that instead of accusing Rose of trying to kill herself?

152

There's no way she would do that."

Jacquie waited for Karen to settle down. "Are you aware that Rose was asked to come to the police station yesterday to talk to Chief Austin?"

Annie shook her head no. "I didn't know that. Did you, Karen?"

Karen looked away, not answering.

"She didn't come in. Chief Austin waited for her, but she blew him off. Do you know why she would do that? What was she afraid of?" Jacquie asked.

Neither woman answered her.

"Annie? Do you know what she was afraid of?"

"Do we need an attorney, Chief Austin? Are you here to arrest us? Because, if you aren't, I'd like both of you to leave," Annie said.

"Do I think you need a lawyer? I don't know, Annie, but you just might. I don't know what's going on with you, but I intend to find out what it is, so you better watch your p's and q's. Getting smart with me isn't helping anything."

Jacquie stood up and headed for the door. "Your attitude sucks, ladies."

"Really?" Annie replied, angrily. "Well, yours would, too, if you had just buried a good friend and almost lost another one and some cop was trying to blame it on you."

"Dear god, Annie. What is wrong with you? We're trying to find out who killed your friend, not blame it on you. But, the fact that you two and your friend, Sandra Peary, won't give us the time of day isn't helping us any. You're hindering our investigation by holding back vital information," Jacquie told her,

153

raising her voice.

"I told you. We don't know anything," Annie exclaimed.

Jacquie turned to Austin. "You ready to leave?" she asked. "Because it stinks in here and I could use some fresh air."

Austin stood and looked at the two women. "I hope you know what you're doing," he told them.

"Don't worry about us," Annie retorted, sarcastically. "We're fine, no thanks to you."

"I'm not your enemy, Annie," Austin said quietly. He glanced over a Jacquie, who was holding the door open, waiting for him to follow her out of the apartment. "One more thing," he said. "Where were you last night?"

Karen gave him a scornful look. "What does that have to do with anything?"

"Annie, where were you?" Austin asked again, ignoring Karen's remark.

"We were at Pat McNally's. Although, I don't see what that has to do with this, either," she replied.

"Who else was there?" Austin inquired.

"No one. Well, Sandra was there, too. It was just the four of us."

"Any special reason you were over at his place?" Austin asked.

"No, there wasn't a special reason. We were just hanging out and helping Pat. It's hard for him to get around. The dumb ass shot himself in the leg, you know. Anyway, we cleaned up his dirty dishes, did a load of washing, had a few drinks, and talked. Nothing special, at all," Annie said.

"I see," Austin said. He looked over at Karen, then, back at Annie. "Let's go," he told Jacquie. "You're right. The air does stink in here."

Chapter Twenty-nine

"Thanks for calling me, George."

"You know me, Augie. I'm not one to stick my nose in where it don't belong. I do my job and keep my mouth shut. However, when I found this, I figured I best give you a call."

"You did the right thing," Austin told him. "Where's the car?"

"Inside the shop. Follow me."

Chief Austin followed George Wendt into one of the bays of the body shop. The trunk was open on the squad car that was in for repairs. "There are a couple of places where I found blood," Wendt said, pointing to the areas he was referring to inside the trunk.

Austin bent forward and took a closer look. "It sure looks like blood," he said. "I need to take a few samples."

"It looks like it's been there for a while," Wendt said.

"It will probably be hard to tell exactly how long with all this hot weather. But I'll send it to forensics to see if they can determine its type."

"It's type?" Wendt asked.

"You know," Austin replied. "Type A or O or whatever."

Wendt shook his head, acknowledging that he understood what Austin meant. "Gotcha," he said.

"I need to get my kit out of my car," Austin said, as he started walking back to his car.

"One more thing, Augie."

"Just a sec. I'll be right back."

Wendt watched Austin retrieve his kit from the squad car and walk back to the open trunk.

"There's something else, Augie. I'm not sure if it means anything but I found a woman's barrette in the trunk, too."

Austin turned towards Wendt, a surprised look on his face. "Where in the trunk?"

"Right there, in the front. It was just lying there. I still have it."

"So, you handled it. Austin declared, frowning.

Wendt grinned. "Nope. When I saw that pretty little thing lying there, I asked myself how it might have got there. You know, being in a cop car and all. It seemed odd to me and I figured you would be interested in knowing about it. I used a little pair of pliers to pick it up and I wrapped it in some toilet paper."

Austin stared at him. "Are you serious?"

"Sure am," Wendt told him, still grinning.

"I'll be sending Jacquie down to go over the car. Until then, it would be best if you and your help let it be."

"I've already told them to stay clear and to keep their mouths shut about this," Wendt told him.

"I'm looking for some help, George. Any chance you want a new job?" Austin asked him, joking.

"Nope. Don't like the hours," Wendt replied.

"Don't blame you."

"There was gunshot powder residue on his right hand. The way the bullet entered indicates that Lober pulled the trigger. There's no doubt in my mind, Augie.

He definitely killed himself."

"There's no sign of foul play?"

"None that I could find," Dr. Severson replied.

"Okay. So, we can close the book on this one."

"And, you're sure he didn't kill the Upton woman?" Severson inquired.

"I'm not one hundred percent sure, but close enough. I can't rule anyone out, but I don't think he did it."

"He had motive."

"I know," Austin replied. "But I don't think he was capable of killing her that way. Right now, Sam is at the bottom of the list."

"Well, she was carrying someone else's kid."

"I know. By the way, I'm sending you some samples of blood that were taken from a trunk of a car. I'd like you to type them for me."

"Who'd they come from?" Severson asked.

"No idea."

"You want to tell me why?"

"I'd like you to check them out first. See if both samples are the same, will you?"

"I can do that. When can I expect them?"

"Jacquie is driving them up to you in a few hours," Austin told him.

"Ah, Jacquie. Perhaps, I'll ask her to lunch."

Jerry, you will do no such thing. She's a nice girl and I don't want you messing with her."

Severson laughed. "I guess it's obvious that you don't trust me when it comes to the ladies."

"Hell no, I don't. Wherever you go, you leave a trail of broken hearts. You leave my Jacquie alone."

"Your Jacquie? That sounds weird."

"I don't care how it sounds, my friend. She's like a daughter to me and I don't want to see her getting hurt."

"You have my word. I'll be a gentleman. Is there anything else you need?"

"That's it for now. Thanks, Jerry. Let me know what you find, okay?"

"Will do."

Jacquie walked in as Austin hung up his phone, grinning from ear to ear. She walked over to her desk, opened the top right drawer, and threw her purse in it. "Coffee still hot, dad?" she asked.

"You were listening," Austin stated. "Shame on you."

"I only heard a little before you hung up," Jacquie told him. "It's good to know you have my back."

"Always," Austin, said, blushing slightly.

"Was that Doc Severson you were talking to?"

"You know it was."

"Why did George Wendt call you?" Jacquie asked.

"He found blood in the trunk of the squad car," Austin told her.

"He what? Why would there be blood in the trunk? That doesn't make any sense."

"Do you know if Pete ever picked up any road kill? He might have thrown a carcass in the trunk and disposed of it later."

"Ya, right. Like Pete would do something like that."

"Just a thought," Austin stated.

"Why don't you just ask him?" Jacquie asked.

"Later, after Severson determines if the blood is human or animal. I want you to drive some samples up to him."

Jacquie grinned. "I'll leave right now."

Austin laughed. "No. You'll leave after you get done checking to see if there's anything else in that trunk that suggests some kind of body was in there. There might be hair or fibers from some clothing. George is holding off doing any more work on the car until you check it out. I want you to go through it with a fine-tooth comb, Jacquie. Don't miss a spot."

"What are you thinking, Chief?"

"I hope to hell I'm wrong, but I. . ." Austin stopped talking and looked away.

"What?"

"He also found a woman's barrette in the trunk."

"I'll check the entire vehicle," Jacquie said, realizing what Austin was getting at.

"Jacquie?"

"What?"

"This goes no further."

"I know," she said.

"I'll check with her dad later. Maybe, he will know if it belonged to her," Austin stated.

"She always wore two and they always matched. Do you remember seeing one on her body when she was found?"

"No."

"Benny might remember. Why don't you ask him?" she asked Austin.

160

"Not yet. I want to find out if the blood is a match first. One step at a time."

"Then, I guess I better get to work. I'll check in before I leave for Portage," Jacquie said.

"Right." Austin reached for his coffee and brought the cup to his mouth. He hesitated for a moment, then, looked over at her. "I want you to come right back after you drop those samples off," he told her.

Jacquie grinned. "Yes, dad."

"And, don't call me dad. I'm Chief dad, to you.

Chapter Thirty

Ronny Ott was sitting across the table from Chief Austin, shoveling eggs, hash brown potatoes, and sausage into his mouth. He put his fork down long enough to take a sip of coffee. Then, he picked up his knife and started spreading strawberry jam on his toast.

Chief Austin lit a cigarette, sat back, and watched him. "That must be pretty damned good," he commented.

Ott looked up at him and grinned. "It sure is. I usually don't eat this fast, but I've got a job at the Corner Drug Store and I'm running late. They sprung a leak and I figure it's gonna take a while to fix it. I need to fuel up before I go there."

"Well, you certainly are doing a good job."

"What did you want to talk to me about?" Ott asked as he shoved another forkful of food into his mouth.

"I'm looking for a part-time cop. I need someone to take Sam's place."

Ott stopped chewing and stared at Austin. "You mean me?"

"I've thought about it. Would you be interested?"

Ott put his fork down and sat back in the booth. "I haven't ever really thought about doing police work. I don't know. I stay fairly busy with my plumbing jobs, but. . ." He hesitated for a moment, thinking. "What are the hours? Didn't Sam work an early shift?"

"Sam worked the four to eight shift. Of course, there are times when you'd need to work overtime, but that doesn't happen too often."

"How's the pay?" Ott asked.

"You'd get the same as what Sam was getting. Are you interested? You'd have to go through some training, of course."

"Can I think about it? I'm a little slow right now and I could use some extra money."

"I couldn't put you on, anyway, until after we solve Debbie's murder."

"I'm a suspect?" Ott asked.

"Not in my book, but you were involved with her once, so I need to get that case closed before you could start. Appearances, and all that shit, you know."

"It might be a little hairy, working with Drollstrom. You know we had a little set to a few days ago."

"I heard about it. I imagine Pete had it coming."

"He did."

"There might be a few occasions when you would have to work together, but that shouldn't happen very often. He is supposed to begin work at eight, but he rarely shows up before nine, so your paths won't cross very often. I don't see that it should be a problem."

Ott looked at Austin's package of cigarettes lying on the table. "Mind if I have a smoke?" he inquired.

Austin pushed the pack closer to Ott. "Help yourself."

Ott lit up a cigarette and inhaled deeply. He sat back as he blew the smoke out. He looked at Austin and sighed. "I've been holding out on you, Chief Austin. There's something I need to tell you about Pete."

163

"What the hell?" Pat McNally uttered. He waited, hoping that whoever was pounding on his front door would go away.

"Pat, are you in there?" Austin shouted. "I need to talk to you."

"It's open," McNally yelled, as he hobbled to the front door.

"I need to talk to you," Austin said again, as he walked into Pat's living room.

"Obviously," McNally said. "What now?"

Chief Austin looked at McNally who was only wearing the bottoms of his pajamas. "Do you work out?" he asked.

McNally gave him a strange look. "That's why you're here?"

Austin laughed. "Sorry. I guess I was just surprised at what good shape you're in."

McNally grinned. "I have to admit that I do a little bench pressing from time to time. Can I get you some coffee?"

"No thanks. Can we sit for a minute? I need to ask you a couple of questions."

"Of course," McNally said.

"You know Ronny Ott, right?"

"Right. We were in school together. He's a hell of a good plumber."

"You know that Ott dated Debbie Nelson?"

"I do. But they broke up quite a while ago," McNally replied, wondering what Austin was getting at.

"They did. About six or seven months ago. You were good friends with Debbie, weren't you?"

"I wouldn't say good friends, but we were friends."

"Well, she was part of your group, wasn't she?" Austin asked.

"My group? I didn't know I have a group."

"Your click, then," Austin commented. "Whatever you call it. I know she spent a lot of time with you."

"She was a good friend to Sandra Peary, who is a good friend of mine. So, ya, I guess you could say that we spent a lot of time together."

"You spend a lot of time with Karen Berke, Annie Berg, and Rose Thomas, too, don't you?"

"I guess," McNally answered. "We're all friends. So, what's the big deal?"

"I'm just trying to figure out the connections."

"By the way, how is Rose doing? Is she any better?" McNally asked, hoping to change the subject.

"I doubt she'll ever get better. It's a damned shame, a young girl like that trying to take her own life. It makes me sick to think about it."

"She tried before, you know."

Austin was quiet for a moment. "I think I know who burned down your farm house," Austin said, abruptly.

"Really."

"Don't you want to know who did it?" Austin asked.

"Of course, I do."

"Does Pete Drollstrom have a problem with you?"

"Why would Pete have a problem with me?"

165

"Because I think he burned down your farm house and I don't know why he would do that if he didn't have some kind of a grudge against you."

McNally's heart started pounding as he wondered how much Austin knew. "I don't have a problem with Pete. Besides, I thought it was some bum who started the fire. There's no way it was Pete."

"How's your leg?" Austin asked, suddenly changing the subject.

"My leg is fine, thanks. Chief, why are you really here?"

"I heard a story today, Pat. I heard that you blackmailed Drollstrom into burning the farm house down. Is that true?"

Pat McNally sat back on the couch and stared at Austin. "I don't know what the hell you're talking about. If Pete told you this garbage, he's full of shit."

"Did you ever find that bullet?" Austin asked.

"We both know that Pete Drollstrom is a piece of shit," McNally said, ignoring his question. "I don't know why he's telling you this crap, but I certainly didn't ask him to burn my house down."

"Did you know there's a rumor that someone is running a cathouse around here and that you might have something to do with it?"

McNally looked like he'd been slapped in the face. "What the fuck is wrong with you? How could you possibly think I'd do something like that?" He sat back and stared at Austin. "What has Pete done now?" he asked, after a few moments.

Austin looked surprised. "What do you mean?"

"Obviously, Pete's in trouble and he's trying to

get the heat off himself by making up shit about me. That's what he always does. It looks like you've fallen for it."

Austin nodded. "You might be right, Pat, if I had heard this from Pete."

"Then, who'd you hear it from? Because, whoever it was, it's all garbage and you know it," McNally said defensively.

"I'd like to hear your side of the story," Austin declared.

"There's no other side because there's no story. It's not true."

"I think there might be some meat on the bone. I got this from a pretty reliable source," Austin said.

McNally glared at him. "Believe what you want. I want you to leave. This is bullshit and I'm done talking to you."

"I have a few more questions."

"No, you don't. We're done here. If you have any more questions, call my attorney."

"I see. So, you have a lawyer. Just who would that be?"

"Cuddehey. I believe you know him."

"I do." Austin stood and headed for the door. "By the way," he said quietly, "don't leave town, Pat. I'll need to talk to you again. Soon."

McNally glared at him. "As I said, talk to my lawyer."

Chapter Thirty-one

"How'd it go?"

"Fine. I handed him the samples and left. He said he'd call you as soon as he found out anything, but it probably won't be until Monday."

"Did he say why it would take so long?" Austin asked Jacquie.

"No. But, I figure it's because it's Saturday afternoon and he doesn't work on weekends."

"Well, he's working today," Austin commented.

"I think he's making an exception. Anyway, that's all he said."

"You haven't said anything to anyone, have you?"

Jacquie shook her head no. "I'm surprised you would even ask me that."

"Sorry. There's a lot going on right now and . . ." Austin stopped talking and looked over as Drollstrom walked through the door.

"Pete," he said, surprised that Drollstrom was still on the job, "it's almost five. What are you doing here?"

"I'm just checking in before I go home. Are you sure you're set for tomorrow?"

"It's covered. Matt and Benny are each doing twelve-hour shifts. They'll call if something comes up that they can't handle."

"When do you figure you'll hire someone to take Sam's place?" Drollstrom asked Austin.

"I'm working on it."

"Do you have anyone in mind?" Drollstrom

asked.

"Why? Do you know someone who might be interested?"

"Not really," Drollstrom answered.

"Well, let me know if you think of someone. You want to get that, Jacquie?" he asked, as the phone rang.

"Columbus Police Department, Officer Gorski here."

Jacquie listened to the caller for a moment and handed the phone to Officer Drollstrom. "It's for you," she told him.

"Who is it?" Drollstrom inquired.

"I haven't the slightest."

Drollstrom grabbed the phone out of her hand. "Drollstrom."

Jacquie watched Drollstrom's face turn red as he listened to the caller.

"No fucking way, man," he said angrily. He listened for a couple of moments and said, "Alright. Twenty minutes."

"Who was that?" Jacquie asked as Drollstrom slammed the phone down.

"No one." He grabbed his hat and headed for the door.

"It wasn't me," Drollstrom said. "How many times do I have to tell you?"

"Pete, Austin thinks that I might have blackmailed you into burning down my farmhouse. And, I'm pretty sure he suspects that I didn't shoot myself and he keeps asking me if I've found the bullet yet."

"What do you mean might have? I don't think there's any might have about it. You did blackmail me."

"Not really. You were just doing me a favor, just like I did you a favor by not telling Austin you shot me. But, if you didn't tell him, who did? There must be somebody that you told because I sure as hell haven't said anything to anyone."

"Ah, fuck," Drollstrom muttered, as he suddenly realized who had talked. "Ott. That fucking Ronny Ott. It has to be him."

"You told Ott? Why would you do that?"

"He's a friend and I needed some advice. At least I thought he was a friend until he decked me. He must have said something to Austin. Shit! Ah, shit."

McNally glared at Drollstrom. "You fucking idiot. Do you have any idea the trouble you've caused?"

Drollstrom looked at him and shrugged. "What's done is done. I guess you're gonna have to find a way to fix it."

"You think? Well, you better find a way, too, because – in case you forgot – you not only shot me but you killed a man when you set that fire."

"I didn't know there was gonna be somebody there. I didn't have a choice." Drollstrom whined.

"Austin asked me if I knew anything about a whorehouse in Columbus. Did that idea come from you, too?"

Drollstrom looked away. "Maybe. I might have said something to Ott."

"You might have?" McNally yelled at him. "My

god, Pete, have you ever used that brain of yours? And, just for your information, there is no whorehouse. Never has been, as far as I know," McNally told him.

Drollstrom smirked. "Sure, McNally," he said, "and, pigs can fly."

McNally stretched out his bad leg and looked at it. "I wonder if I'll ever be able to walk again without a limp," he commented.

"It hasn't even been a week," Drollstrom said. "You've got to give it some time to heal."

"Well, it seems like a hell of a lot longer than that."

"What did you do with the bullet?" Drollstrom asked.

"Nice try, Pete."

"You got any beer?" Drollstrom asked.

"I do, but you're leaving, so forget it. I've got some calls to make."

"Then, we're done here," Drollstrom stated, as he stood up and headed for the door. "What are you gonna do, Pat?"

"I'm not sure. One more question, though, before you leave."

Drollstrom glanced over at him, waiting.

"Are you positive that Ott is the only one you said anything to? And, don't lie to me, Pete. This is important. I've got to know what I'm dealing with."

"He was the only one. I swear."

"You're sure?" McNally inquired.

"I'm sure. Why? What are you thinking?"

"I'm thinking that you owe me another favor."

171

"Bullshit, I do. I told you – we're even," Drollstrom shouted.

"We'll see."

"No seeing about it," Drollstrom yelled.

"Why did Ott deck you? You never said."

"It's none of your fucking business, Pat."

"You must have really stepped out of line for him to hit a cop. Especially, a cop in uniform and in front of all those witnesses. Come on, tell me. Whatcha say to him?"

"Fuck you," Drollstrom yelled as he opened the front door and walked out of the house.

McNally grinned. "How come you didn't arrest him," he shouted to Drollstrom as he walked down the sidewalk toward his car.

Drollstrom suddenly stopped halfway to his car, turned, and walked back into McNally's house. "Pat," he yelled.

McNally, who was walking into the kitchen, looked over his shoulder. "Did you forget something?" he asked, surprised to see that Drollstrom had walked back into the house.

"You're right," Drollstrom said. "This mess with Ott is my fault. That has to be who Austin got his information from. He's the only one I mentioned anything to. I'll take care of him."

"What do you mean, you'll take care of him?" McNally asked.

"I'll talk to him and find out just how much he told Austin. From what you've told me, it sounds like he pretty much repeated everything I told him. However, at this point, it's his word against mine. As far as I know, there's no evidence against me or you."

McNally stared at him, wondering what Drollstrom was up to. "What exactly are you planning on doing, Pete?"

"Like I said, I'll talk to him."

"And, what makes you think he'll want to talk to you? The last time you saw him, you two got into a fight. Or, have you forgotten?"

"Of course, I haven't forgotten. But I know him. I'll apologize and he'll get over it. Before you know it, we'll be best buds again. Believe me, I know what I'm doing. Just let me talk to him before you do anything."

"I don't know, Pete," McNally replied. "You sure you won't fuck this up?"

Drollstrom looked McNally in the eyes. "Leave this to me," he said, dead serious. "I know what has to be done."

Chapter Thirty-two

"How much longer do you think it will take?" Sandra asked Pat.

"I might have had a check coming by now if that moron hadn't killed someone," Pat told her. "With a death being involved, it could take months before it's settled."

"So, what are we gonna do about the restaurant? What if someone else buys it? What are we gonna do then?"

"Relax. I've got an appointment with the realtor to check it out tomorrow. I'll see how much wiggle room there is on the asking price. You know - feel him out a little. I think you ladies have saved enough for the down payment and we'll mortgage the balance."

"No way," Sandra said, raising her voice. "The whole idea was to go into this debt-free. Now, you're talking about getting a mortgage. You know very well that no bank is going to loan us money. For crying out loud, Pat, none of us have a job. I don't understand your thinking."

"Let me finish. I'll get the loan, so it's in my name. You guys don't have to be involved in that. I'll be getting money from the sale of the farm and the investigation into the fire can't go on forever. As soon as I get the check from the insurance company, I'll pay off the mortgage."

"I don't think that will cut it. I don't think the bank will give you a mortgage on speculation. There's no guarantee that the insurance claim will be paid or that the farm will sell. I'm pretty sure the banks aren't loaning money to anyone without a steady income," Sandra said.

"I have a steady income," Pat told her.

"Since when? Except for pimping us out, I've never known you to have a real job."

Pat gave her a dirty look. "I'm not a pimp, Sandra, and you know it. I'm a businessman."

Sandra chuckled. "Right. And, I'm the Queen of Sheba," she said.

"I do have a steady income," Pat said, starting to get upset.

"Since when?"

Pat pursed his lip, thinking before he answered. "When my grandfather died, he left me an inheritance. It's in a trust and I get more than enough to cover a mortgage every month. Getting a loan from the bank isn't going to be a problem."

"But, then, everything will be in your name. You'll be the sole owner," Sandra stated, frowning. "I don't think I like that idea and I don't think the others will either."

"Do you have a better idea? Because, if you do, I'd like to hear it. I'm trying to work this out and you're basically accusing me of trying to cheat you. What the fuck, Sandra. You know me better than that."

"I'm sorry. I just don't like the idea."

"As soon as I pay off the mortgage, I'll sign the restaurant over to you guys. We'll do our original agreement. Nothing is going to change. It's just going to take a little longer than we planned, so stop worrying."

"I guess it will be okay," Sandra told him, as she

put her hand under the covers and started to rub Pat's chest. "Are you going to church this morning?"

"I guess," Pat said and smiled as Sandra's hand slid a little lower.

"Early or late service?"

Pat grinned. "I'm pretty sure it's gonna be the late one."

Catherine Austin, looking concerned, put the phone down on the kitchen counter and walked into the living room. She motioned to Augie to turn the volume down on the radio.

He reached over and turned the dial, lowering the sound to almost a whisper. "What?" he asked, obviously aggravated at being interrupted.

"The phone," Catherine said softly.

"Tell whoever it is that I'll call them back," Augie told her and reached over to turn the volume back up.

"Augie," Catherine said, "it's Dr. Severson. He said it's important."

"It's Jerry?" he asked, looking surprised. "What could he want?"

"He's waiting, dear. Should I tell him that you'll call him back?"

"No, I'll take it," he told her, pushed himself out of his favorite chair, and went into the kitchen to answer the call.

"This better be good, Jerry. You're interrupting the Braves' game."

"I'm done checking the samples that Jacquie brought in yesterday and I figured you want this

176

information now, Augie."

"That was fast."

"You know me. I couldn't rest with this hanging over my head, so I decided to come into the lab this morning and run the tests."

"What did you find?" Austin asked, holding his breath.

"First of all, the blood that was found in the trunk of the squad car is human. Second, the hair that Jacquie found in the trunk is human. And, third, the two strands of hair and two blood samples that were found in the back seat of the squad car are human and match the ones found in the trunk."

"So, this means that the same person was in the car and the trunk," Austin commented.

"Well, not exactly," Severson declared. "It simply means that something with the person's hair and/or blood on it was in the vehicle. It wouldn't have had to be at the same time and it could have been transferred from an article of clothing or something similar."

"So, if, let's say, a sweater was tossed in the trunk with blood and hair on it, it could have left trace evidence."

"Right. Just finding the blood and hair doesn't necessarily mean that there was a person there. Although, I would say that the blood had to be pretty fresh to leave that type of a stain. If I had to guess, I'd say the blood stains had been there for about a week. Of course, there's no way to know how long the hair had been there."

"But you would agree that finding human blood and hair in a trunk is unusual, wouldn't you?

Especially, a police car."

"I would definitely say it's unusual finding blood in the trunk of any vehicle," Severson replied.

"Okay. So far, so good. Is there anything else?"

"There is. I checked the blood samples against the samples that I took from the Upton woman. They're all a match."

"No fucking way!" Austin yelled out, then, immediately looked around to see if his wife had heard him.

Catherine was staring at him, a shocked look on her face.

"Sorry," he mouthed to her. "Go on, Jerry."

"The strands of hair that were found came from the Upton woman. In other words, Augie, everything that was delivered to me for testing came from the Upton woman. I hope this helps," Severson said, "I'll go over everything again tomorrow and finish up, but I wanted to get these results to you right away. I'll send you a written report sometime later this week."

"Sounds good. Thanks for getting this information to me so fast."

"No problem. I'll let you get back to your baseball game."

"Are you still drinking that high-priced scotch you like so much?" Austin asked him.

"I am. And, I expect to be getting a bottle of it the next time I see you," Severson told him, laughing.

Chapter Thirty-three

"God, I hate Monday mornings," Jacquie declared as she walked into the police station.

"Doesn't everyone?" Austin replied. "Did you have a good weekend?"

"I guess; if you can call Sunday a weekend. A few of us drove over to Beaver Dam and did some bar hopping Saturday night. I pretty much spent yesterday recovering."

"I remember those days," Austin said. "And, I'm glad they're over." He looked up as Officer Drollstrom walked in. "Morning, Pete," he said, acknowledging him.

"Morning, Chief. Jacquie. How you guys doing this morning?"

Jacquie glanced over at Austin, surprised. Something's up, Jacquie thought. "We're fine, Pete," she told him.

"Anything new?" Drollstrom asked.

"Like what?" Jacquie replied.

"Like, my dad wants to know if you've solved the two murders you've been working on?"

"Jacquie, I'd like you to check in on Rose Thomas sometime today," Austin said, ignoring Drollstrom. "Talk to the doctor and see if anything has changed."

"Sure thing," Jacquie told him.

"Also, I think Arlis Upton's father is at home. I want you to show him that object we found and see if he recognizes it. You should probably do that now before he heads out for the week."

"I'm on it," she said, grabbing her hat and heading out the door.

"What object?" Drollstrom asked.

"Pete, you and I need to talk," Austin said.

"About what?" Drollstrom asked.

"Sit down."

"What's going on?"

"I've got some questions you need to answer, so you best sit down."

"Can I grab a cup of coffee, first?"

"Help yourself."

Officer Drollstrom was fighting to control his anger. For almost fifteen minutes, Chief Austin had been questioning him about the fire at McNally's farm, and the shooting of Pat McNally.

"You know that Ott and I had a disagreement, don't you?" Drollstrom asked. "Did it ever occur to you that he made that shit up to get even with me?"

"No," Austin said. "I believed every word he said."

"Let me make this clear. I did not shoot Pat McNally in the leg. I did not burn down his farmhouse. Pat and I don't have a problem with each other. There's no reason I would do any of that shit. I don't know what you want me to say, but I sure as hell am not going to admit to something I didn't do."

"More coffee?" Austin asked him, as he walked over to refill his cup.

"No, I don't want more coffee," Drollstrom answered. He watched Austin fill his cup, return to his desk, and sit down.

Austin lit up a cigarette, took a deep drag, and blew out the smoke. "Did you ever date Arlis Upton?" he asked.

Drollstrom's face turned beet red, as he dug his fingernails into the palms of his hands. He gave Austin a dirty look and started to stand.

"Sit down," Austin told him, "and answer my question. Did you ever date Arlis Upton?"

"She was Sam's girl," Drollstrom told him.

"That's not what I asked. I asked you if you ever dated her."

"No, I didn't date her."

"Did you ever arrest her?"

"For what?" Drollstrom asked.

"Did you ever arrest her?"

"No."

"Do you know of any reason why she would have been in the squad car that you use?"

Drollstrom looked away. "No."

"Did you ever see or put any articles of her clothing or other objects that belonged to her, in the back seat of that car?"

"No."

"Did you ever see or put any articles of her clothing or other objects that belonged to her, in the trunk of that vehicle?"

"What the . . ."

"Answer the question, Pete. Did you?"

"No."

"So, you never went out with her and you never arrested her. You never saw any object or clothing that belonged to her inside the squad or in the trunk of the squad car, that you drive, while on duty. Is that what you're telling me?"

"Exactly."

Austin sat back in his chair and stared at Drollstrom. "Do you want to change any of your answers?"

"No, I don't want to change any of my answers," Pete replied, sarcastically.

"We found hair and blood evidence in the back seat and trunk of your squad car, Pete. The tests show that these samples belong to Arlis Upton. Perhaps, you'd like to explain how they got there."

Drollstrom thought for a moment, then, grinned. "Of course, I can explain it."

"You can?" Austin asked, surprised.

"It's a known fact that she occasionally rode with Sam while he was patrolling. That's probably how that evidence got in the car."

"You drive that car, Pete. Sam didn't use that car."

"But, he did," Drollstrom said, excitedly. "We all switch cars from time to time. Just because that's the one I usually drive, doesn't mean no one else drives it. That explains everything. Sam killed Arlis. It makes sense now. Don't you see, Chief? She was pregnant and it wasn't his. He was angry because she had messed around and he killed her. He probably put her body in the trunk until he had a chance to throw it in the river." He sat back, crossed his arms over his chest, and smiled. "Looks like I just solved that murder case, doesn't it?" he said, looking pleased with himself.

Austin looked stunned. "Do you actually believe that shit you just said? Arlis Upton was raped, Pete. And, I think it was you that raped her. I think it was your child she was carrying. Sam was planning on marrying her. He didn't kill her. You did, because you were afraid she'd tell Sam what happened."

"Now, you're accusing me of rape?" Drollstrom shouted. "Why don't you just pin every crime that's taken place in Columbus on me? That would be an easy way to clear the books, wouldn't it?"

"Perhaps, it would," Austin answered. "But I don't do things that way."

Drollstrom smirked. "You have no proof that I've done anything wrong. You're grabbing at straws. Tell me, Chief Austin, do I need an attorney? Should I have my dad call Cuddehey? Because I'm done answering these ridiculous allegations." Pete stood up and walked towards the door. "I've got a job to do. If you want to talk to me about this shit again, call my attorney."

Austin pushed Drollstrom through the entrance that led to the arena, causing him to fall to his knees. The crowd cheered when they saw him, anxious for the bloody battle to begin. Drollstrom rose and picked up the sword that lay at his feet. He turned, his face wet with sweat, and gazed at his surroundings.

The cry of the crowd rose, as two lions, thirsty for blood, came towards him. Drollstrom knew he was doomed. He turned, fear spreading across his face, and looked at Austin. "Why?" he screamed. "Why?"

Austin smiled, watching as the lions crouched low, studying their prey, preparing to attack.

Suddenly, just as the lions leaped forward, Drollstrom turned the sword in towards his body and drove it into his chest. He sunk to the ground, unaware of the boos coming from the crowd, as the lions started ripping the flesh from his dying body.

Austin reached into his shirt pocket, pulled out a cigarette, and lit it. "That takes care of that," he uttered to himself, as he blew smoke into the air.

"Where are you going?" Austin asked.

"To see my father," Drollstrom yelled.

Chief Austin sat back, took a sip of his lukewarm coffee, and watch Drollstrom walk out the door.

A few minutes later, Jacquie strolled into the police station, a smile on her face.

"It's hers?" Austin asked.

"It's hers," Jacquie told him.

"Pete killed her," Austin stated.

"I figured he did. Can you prove it?"

"Not yet," Austin replied. "But, I will, Jacquie. One way or the other, that bastard is going to jail."

Chapter Thirty-four

Rose slowly opened her eyes, wondering where she was. The light hurt her eyes and she blinked, trying to filter out the brightness. She felt, rather than saw, the tubes, filled with liquids, that were keeping her alive.

A noise caught Rose's attention. She glanced across the room and saw her mother sitting in a chair next to a window. She watched as her mother slowly flipped the pages of a magazine. A solitary tear rolled down Rose's cheek. She closed her eyes and escaped, once more, into nothingness.

Mrs. Thomas sighed, as she closed the latest copy of the Life magazine. She was tired and she wished she could leave the hospital and go home.

She glanced over at her daughter, wondering how long it would be before the cost of keeping her alive would bankrupt the family. Just fucking die, will you, Mrs. Thomas thought and immediately felt remorse at thinking such a horrible thing. She walked over to the side of Rose's bed and took her daughter's hand. "I'm sorry, Rose," she whispered. "I didn't mean it."

"Oh," she cried out, as she felt Rose squeeze her hand. Her heart started to race with excitement. "Can you hear me, Rose?"

She looked at her daughter's face, willing her to open her eyes. "Rose, can you hear me?" she asked again, raising her voice. "Say something."

"Mrs. Thomas, are you okay?"

Mrs. Thomas glanced towards the door. "She

heard me," she told the nurse, excitedly. "I was talking to her and she squeezed my hand."

"I'm sorry, but that's not possible. It was probably just a spasm."

"I know she heard me," Mrs. Thomas said angrily, raising her voice. "I want you to call the doctor right now and tell him."

"Can I get you anything? A cup of coffee or some juice, maybe?"

Mrs. Thomas stared at her. "No, thank you. I'm sorry I yelled at you. It's just that I'm so tired," she said after a few moments.

"Of course, you are. Why don't you go home for a while and take a nap? I'll keep an eye on Rose."

"I could use some rest. You promise you'll watch over her?"

"I promise," the nurse told her. "Now, you go home. I'll call you if anything changes."

Mrs. Thomas picked up her purse and headed for the door. She turned and looked at her daughter. "Bye, Rose," she said softly. "I'll be back soon."

"That's all?" Sandra asked Pat.

"That's all, baby. We're in business," he told her.

"What's wrong with the place?"

"What do you mean – what's wrong? Nothing's wrong. I'm just good at what I do."

"Pat, they came down almost a fourth of the asking price. I don't care how good you are, that's not normal."

"They want out, that's all. That place has been on the market for a long time. It's costing the owners a fortune and they have their eye on a place down south somewhere. Florida, I think. Anyway, I made an offer, the realtor called them and they accepted. They didn't even try to counter."

"When will you talk to Hobson about the loan?" Sandra inquired.

"Probably tomorrow. It won't be a problem getting a mortgage. We'll be putting almost a third down."

"No, we won't," Sandra told him. "We're going to put the minimum amount down, which will leave us with enough money to start remodeling. Then, when you get all your money, you can pay it off and we'll own it free and clear."

"It may be a while before I sell the farm and I'm still not sure how long before I get the insurance check. I'm going to be carrying a pretty big mortgage payment if we only put the minimum amount down, Sandra."

"Nothing is coming out of your pocket up front, Pat, and I know for a fact that you've got the money. So, quite whining, will you?"

He gave her a dirty look. "God, you can be a bitch sometimes," he told her.

"Ya? Well, fuck you."

Pat grinned. "Where's the money for the down payment?" he asked.

"I've got it, don't worry."

"I'm not worried, but I have to show the bank where the money came from. I'll be taking it out of my savings, so you'll need to reimburse me right away."

"How much?" Sandra asked him.

"I'll do the numbers tonight and let you know." He reached over and started stroking her thigh. "I love summer," he stated.

"Why's that?"

"Because short shorts make everything so accessible," he told her, as he moved his finger up her leg.

"I have to go," Sandra said. "I'm meeting Karen and Annie."

Pat tucked his finger under her panties and slowly moved it toward the inside of her thigh. "Are you coming back?" he asked, softly.

Sandra moaned, as his fingers gently started caressing her.

Pat grinned, as he pulled her to him. "You sure you want to leave?"

Suddenly, Sandra pushed him away and jumped up off the couch. "You are such a bastard."

Pat sat back and watched her walk toward the door. "What am I supposed to do with this?" he asked, grinning, as he looked down his crotch.

Sandra turned and laughed. "Maybe you should give Rosy Palm and her five sisters a call."

"Phone call, Augie," Catherine Austin called to her husband. "It's Dr. Poszert."

Austin glanced at the clock, noting that it was almost ten-thirty. He got up, turned off the television, and walked into the kitchen. He looked questioningly at his wife. She shrugged, indicating that she didn't know what the call was about.

"I bet the Thomas girl died," he whispered to her,

as he picked up the receiver. "Austin here, Doc." He listened for a moment, shaking his head up and down. "Right. I'll see you in the morning."

Catherine watched as her husband hung up the phone. He sat down at the kitchen table, looking perplexed. "Isn't that the damndest thing," he stated.

What is, dear?" his wife asked.

"Rose Thomas just came out of her coma and she's talking her head off."

Catherine clapped her hands together in joy, a big smile on her face. "Why, that's wonderful," she exclaimed.

"Everyone thought that she was brain dead," Austin declared, looking shocked. "How could this happen?"

Catherine bent down and kissed him on top of his head. "Miracles do happen, Augie. We all know that God answers prayers. I'd say that someone was praying really hard for her to live. It's a downright miracle."

Austin smiled. "You're right. It is. This calls for a beer."

Catherine gave him a strange look. "But you've already had one beer tonight. Do you think that's a good idea?"

Augie laughed. "Not only is it a good idea, but I think you should have one, too."

"Oh, no. I couldn't drink a whole bottle of beer, but I'll have a sip of yours if that's okay."

"You can have two sips if you want," he told her as he opened the refrigerator door.

189

Chapter Thirty-five

At six forty-five on Tuesday morning, Chief Austin stood in the entrance to Rose Thomas' hospital room and stared at an empty bed. He turned and walked down the corridor to the nurse's station, only to find that no one was there. He waited a few moments, then, turned and walked back towards the empty room.

"She's gone."

Austin jumped. "Crap, you scared me," he said, turning to the nurse who was standing behind him. "You need to put cleats on your shoes so you don't scare the bejesus out of people."

"Sorry."

"Did you move Rose to a different room?"

"I'm sorry if I didn't make myself clear," the nurse said. "I meant she died, Chief Austin. A couple of hours ago."

"I don't understand. I got a call from Dr. Poszert last night telling me that she was awake and talking. What happened?"

"I'm not sure. You'll need to talk to Dr. Poszert about that."

"Were you here when she died?"

"No. I'm just starting my shift."

"Where's Dr. Poszert? I need to talk to him."

"He's not in yet."

Austin paused, trying to calm down and absorb the news. He took a deep breath and let out the air. "Here's what I need from you," he told the nurse, after a few moments. "I want the names of everyone who was on duty last night that had any contact with Rose. I want the names of any family members that were here. In other words, I need to know everybody that she might have talked to before she died. Every single person," Austin said, talking too loudly. "Do you understand me?"

"Please lower your voice, Chief Austin," the nurse requested.

Austin looked away. "Sorry. I need that list as soon as possible," he said softly.

"I understand."

"What doctor was on duty when she died?" Austin asked.

"I have to check. Like I told you, I just got here a few minutes ago."

"Do you know where Rose's parents are?" Austin inquired.

"No, sir, I don't."

"You have an hour. Deputy Gorski will pick up the list in an hour."

"I'm not sure that's enough time, Chief Austin. I have patients to attend to and they come first."

"Right now, this comes first. Understand?" he asked her. "I don't care how you do it, just get it done."

Austin turned and walked towards the elevator, his fists clenched in anger. He turned around and shouted to the nurse, who was still standing there watching him walk away. "You have Dr. Poszert call me the minute he comes in," he called to her, as he pushed the down button.

"I know," Austin said into the phone. "I will. Do

you think flowers would help? Or, maybe a box of chocolates?" He looked at Jacquie, who was sitting at her desk, listening to his conversation with Dr. Poszert. She was grinning.

"Not funny," he mouthed at her.

"When?" he asked Dr. Poszert. "Fine. Candy it is. I'll see you then."

"It sounds like you pissed off the good doctor. What the hell did you do?"

"It seems I upset one of the nurses and he thinks she's due an apology and some candy."

"Well, did you?"

"Did I what?" Austin asked, looking confused.

"Did you upset her?"

"I might have raised my voice a little, but I didn't mean anything by it. I don't know why women are so sensitive," he told Jacquie.

Jacquie laughed. "You've been married for years. I would think you'd know better."

"You need to run up to the hospital and pick up a list from that nurse," Austin told Jacquie.

"What's her name?"

Austin shrugged. "I didn't get her name. She's short and has blond hair and could lose about fifty pounds."

"That's Marjorie," Jacquie declared. "What list am I picking up?"

"It's a list of everyone that Rose talked to after she woke up and before she died. When Doc Poszert called me last night, he told me that she was talking her head off. I need to find out what she said."

"When are you meeting with him?"

"Around one. Right now, though, I'm going to talk to Rose's parents."

"Good luck with that," Jacquie told him.

"Why? Is there a problem?"

"He's a drinker. I just hope he's still sober when you get there."

"It's only nine o'clock," Austin observed.

"It's five o'clock somewhere," Jacquie replied.

"Is that everything?" Austin asked.

Mrs. Thomas reached for another tissue and blew her nose. She shook her head yes, and glanced over at her husband. "That's all I remember her talking about, Charles. What about you?"

Mr. Thomas reached for the bottle sitting on the table and poured another drink into his glass. He looked up at Austin. "You sure you don't want one?" he asked.

"No thanks. I'm on duty," Austin said.

"Well, I'm having another one," Mr. Thomas declared. "And, nobody better try to stop me," he uttered, looking at his wife.

"Getting drunk isn't going to bring Rose back," Mrs. Thomas said softly.

Chief Austin watched Rose's parents, wondering how Catherine and he would act if it had been their daughter who died. It's true, he thought, that everyone deals with grief in their own way.

"I know you're going through a lot right now, Mrs. Thomas, but could we go over it one more time? I just have this feeling that something isn't adding up."

"I don't know what more you want me to say,

Chief Austin. Most of what Rose said didn't make much sense. We didn't have a normal conversation."

"And, you were there the entire time she was awake?"

"I was. It might have been fifteen or twenty minutes before Charles showed up," she told Austin.

"You called Charles?" Austin asked.

"Right after Rose woke up. It was the first thing I did."

"Tell me again what she said about Debbie," Austin said.

"She said she was sorry for what happened to Debbie and that no one was supposed to get hurt. I don't know what that means. It was all so confusing."

"Those were her exact words? That no one was supposed to get hurt?"

"Well, not exact, but close. I think that's what she meant. She was doing a lot of rambling."

"What else?"

"I told you already."

"Please, Mrs. Thomas, humor me."

Ruth Thomas looked annoyed. "She said ding dong bell, dead man's in the well. She laughed when she said that. She also told me that she has a lot of money.

"And, that we're all going to be rich," Charles Thomas said sarcastically. "Don't forget that, Ruth. She was excited that we were going to be rich. God, I've never heard such dribble."

"It must have been important or she wouldn't have said it, Charles," Mrs. Thomas said to her husband.

"It's all important," Austin told them. "Please continue."

"I remember her saying something about not having intercourse with someone. She said a name but I couldn't make it out,"

"Do you remember her exact sentence?"

"I do. But I can't repeat it.

"Please, Mrs. Thomas. This is important."

"She said that he told her he would never fuck her," Mrs. Thomas said, looking embarrassed. "Sorry," she said, looking at Austin. "I don't usually use that kind of language."

"No, don't be sorry. You're doing great. Are you sure you don't remember the man's name?"

"No, I didn't understand what she said."

"What else do you remember?"

"Let me see." She thought for a moment. "Sandra's always bossing me." Mrs. Thomas looked over at Austin. "How is this helping you? It doesn't make any sense."

"But it does help. All these things she said were important to her. It might help me find a reason why she died."

"It's just rambling. After a while, I just tuned her out. She wasn't right in the head," Mr. Thomas said, disgustingly.

"Did she say anything about Pete Drollstrom?"

Mrs. Thomas gave him a strange look. "Officer Drollstrom?"

"Yes. Do you remember her mentioning his name?"

Mrs. Thomas shook her head no.

195

"What about Pat McNally?"

Again, Mrs. Thomas shook her head no.

"Yes, she did," Mr. Thomas said, as he took a sip of his drink. "She mentioned him in that dumb poem. Remember, Ruth? That rhyme that she said over and over. 'Ding dong bell, dead man's in the well, Pat pushed him in, and now we're all in hell.' For Pete's sake, she said it more than once. How could you not remember that?"

"Of course. Now I remember," Mrs. Thomas stated. "I was only remembering the first part. She did say that a number of times."

Chief Austin stared at Charles Thomas. "You're sure that's what she said? Pat pushed him in?"

"I'll never forget it. I can't get the damn thing out of my head. How can you even think that meant something? It was all total nonsense if you ask me."

"Did she say anything about why she took so many pills?"

"Chief Austin, we asked her all the questions. We didn't get one straight answer. It was all mumble-jumble. It's a blessing that she died. She had severe brain damage. According to Dr. Poszert, she never should have come out of that coma. He can't give us a reasonable explanation of why she did. He said that we'll probably never know. Anyway, what difference does it make what she said or didn't say? She's gone," Mr. Thomas said. He put his head in his hands and started sobbing.

"I'll leave you to it, then," Austin said, getting up from the table. "Again, please accept my sincere condolences on your loss."

"Thank you," Mrs. Thomas replied.

"Let me know if there's anything you need," Austin said, as he turned to leave.

"Chief Austin?"

"Yes?"

"Do you think Rose committed suicide?"

Austin shook his head no. "Most likely it was an accident. I don't think she wanted to die," he lied.

Mrs. Thomas reached over and took her husband's hand. "Thank you," she said. "We're Catholic, you know and suicide is a sin. We were so worried that her soul would be lost forever. At least, now we can put her to rest, knowing that she will go to heaven."

Chapter Thirty-six

"Pete," Chief Austin asked his officer, "have you ever been out to the old McNally farm?"

Drollstrom, who was at his desk reading the latest edition of the Columbus Journal, looked over at Austin. "Not that I recall," he lied and looked away.

"You sure?"

I don't do farms, Chief," he said, jokingly. "I hate pigs. They stink."

"I'd like you to drive out there and check something out for me."

"What's that?" Drollstrom asked.

"I want to know if there's a well on the property."

"I think most farms have wells, don't they?" Drollstrom asked, smirking.

"I think so. But some are the kind with pump handles. What I need to know is if there's a well out there with an opening big enough for a person to climb into. You know, one that looks like a wishing well, with a bucket attached to it."

"What?" Drollstrom chuckled. "You're not serious?"

"I'm dead serious. Take a drive out there and let me know what you find."

"Right now?"

"Do you have something better to do?"

Drollstrom stood up and stretched. "Nope. I'll see you in a bit."

Austin and Jacquie watched Drollstrom walk out of the police station. As soon as he was out of sight, Jacquie looked questioningly at her boss. "What's that all about?"

"Ding dong bell," Austin recited. "Dead man's in the well."

"Are you okay, Chief?" Jacquie asked, laughing.

"Pat pushed him in; now we're all in hell."

"Little Miss Muffet, sat on a tuffet. . ."

"I'm serious," Austin interrupted. "That's one of the crazy things Rose said before she died. What do you think it means?"

Jacquie sat back, softly mouthing the rhyme. Suddenly, she grinned. "Pat killed someone and threw him down the well on his farm. Rose either saw it or knew about it." She hesitated a moment. "They all know about it, don't they? Annie, Karen, and Sandra know what happened to Debbie. Rose knew, too. That makes sense, doesn't it, considering all the secrecy about Debbie's death and no one telling us anything."

Austin didn't say anything. He watched Jacquie as she tried to put the pieces together in her mind.

"Now we're all in hell," she said softly, emphasizing the 'all'. "She could have meant that Pat and the dead man -whoever that is - and her were all going to go to hell."

"Possibly," Austin commented.

"Rose didn't keep her appointment with you," Jacquie continued. "She was afraid of something. Was it you? Was she afraid that you'd get her to talk and spill the beans about what happened to Debbie? Is that why she took a bottle of sleeping pills and killed herself? Or," Jacquie paused and looked up at the ceiling, thinking. "Or, did someone murder her to keep her from talking?" She looked smug, as she glanced

199

over at Austin. "That's it, isn't it?"

"Pretty much." Austin agreed.

"Karen, Annie, and Sandra are all part of it, aren't they?"

Austin looked exasperated. "Except we don't know what the 'it' is and it doesn't explain what happened to Debbie or who is in the well. If there even is a body in the well."

"Maybe, the 'it' is a house of ill repute. Do you think that McNally could have been running one out of the farmhouse?"

"I don't know, Jacquie. That whorehouse thing is just gossip. I'm not sure there even is one."

"Ronny Ott said that Pete told him that he shot McNally out there. Perhaps, Pete was a customer and something went wrong and Pete shot McNally. It could have been an accident. Or, maybe, Pete got into a fight with someone else and shot that guy. Pat might have thrown the guy down the well to cover it up," Jacquie stated.

"Ott did tell me that Pete shot McNally, but Rose's poem says that Pat pushed a dead man in, not Pete.

Jacquie frowned. "Well, I'll lay you odds that Pete's involved somehow."

"I'd bet on it, too," Austin answered. "By the way, have you seen Ott around town? He was supposed to get back to me yesterday about the job."

"Nope, I haven't seen him. He's probably just busy," Jacquie replied. "How long do you think Pete will be gone?"

Austin checked his watch. "It's two-thirty now. I

200

figure we won't see him again until quitting time."

"What are you planning to do if there is a well out there?" Jacquie inquired.

"I'll need to get a search warrant, which could prove a little difficult. All I've got to go on right now is a dead woman's crazy rantings. I might need a little more than that."

"You've gotten them for fewer reasons than that," Jacquie commented.

Exactly thirty minutes later, Officer Drollstrom strolled into the police station. He looked around the room, saw it was empty, and walked over to the safe. He turned the handle and swore. It was locked. One of these days it will be unlocked and I'll get my gun back, he thought.

"Something you need, Pete?" Austin asked, as he walked into the room and saw Drollstrom standing in front of the safe.

Drollstrom jumped. "Shit! You scared me."

"What are you doing?"

"Nothing," Drollstrom told him, as he walked over to his desk and sat down.

"Did you find a well?" Austin asked him.

"I did. It wasn't hard to find. It's right across from where the house used to be, on the other side of the driveway."

"And?" Austin prompted.

"And, its opening is big enough for a person to fit through," Pete said. "Why do you want to know, anyway?"

"I have something else I'd like you to do," Austin

told him, ignoring his question.

Drollstrom looked up at the clock on the wall. "It's getting close to quitting time. Can't this wait until tomorrow?"

Austin felt his ears getting hot, an indication that his blood pressure was rising. He took a deep breath and slowly let out the air. "I want you to drive over to Ott's place and see if he's home," he said quietly, keeping his temper under control.

Drollstrom's heart started to pound. He bent down and pretended to tie his shoe, hoping that Austin wouldn't notice the uneasy look on his face. "Why not just call him?" he asked, still bent over.

"I tried. There's no answer."

"He's probably out on a job," Drollstrom commented, as he sat back up, feeling more in control.

"That might be, but his mom doesn't know where he is either, and he always checks in with her. Just drive over and make sure that nothing has happened to him."

"It's a waste of time," Drollstrom whined. "He's fine."

"Just do it, Pete," Austin said. "God, just once I'd like to ask you to do something without getting an argument."

"I'm not arguing," Drollstrom told him. "I just think it's a waste of time."

"I'll be the judge of what's a waste of time. Just do it, will you?"

Chapter Thirty-seven

"When was the last time you talked to him?" Chief Austin asked Ronny's mom, Gladys Ott.

Mrs. Ott reached for the percolator and poured herself another cup of coffee. "Can I top off your coffee?" she asked Austin.

Austin shook his head no, "Thanks, but I'm fine." He looked down at his coffee cup, which was almost full, wondering if he would be able to finish it. I've had some bad coffee, he thought, but this is strong enough to choke a horse. He looked at Mrs. Ott, waiting for an answer to his question.

Mrs. Ott pulled out a chair and sat down. She took a sip of coffee and looked over at Austin. "I remember Ronny calling me late Saturday afternoon. He sounded fine and he didn't say anything to me about leaving town."

"We've checked his house and it doesn't look like any of his clothes are missing. His truck is there, so he must still be in town. Are you sure he didn't say anything else? Did he mention any plans for the night? Perhaps, he had a date?" Austin inquired.

Mrs. Ott took another sip of coffee. Suddenly, she smiled. "He did," she said, suddenly. "I forgot."

"He did what?" Austin inquired

"You know he had a fight with Pete Drollstrom, don't you?"

"I do," Austin replied, wishing she'd get to the point.

"Well, he told me that Pete called him and apologized for hitting him. He said he wanted to take

Ronny out and buy him a drink. I think he mentioned that they were going to meet at The Shamrock Tavern. Does that help?"

"It does and I'll check it out. In the meanwhile, if you hear from Ronny, please call me."

"He told me you offered him a job," Mrs. Ott stated.

"I did. I talked to him on Saturday about it. I've been waiting to hear back from him."

"I think he's going to take it," Mrs. Ott said. "He told me he was interested in working for you. He has a lot of respect for you, Chief Austin."

"Thank you." Austin stood up and walked towards the kitchen door. "Don't get up," he told Mrs. Ott, as he opened the door, anxious to get out into the fresh air. "Please let me know if you hear from him," he said.

"This isn't like him, you know," Mrs. Ott declared. "He's very dependable. I hope this doesn't hurt his chances of getting the job."

"Not at all," Austin called to her, as he ran down the back steps and hurried to his car.

Chief Austin drove out towards Astico, planning to stop at The Shamrock Tavern and talk to Mrs. Franz. If Pete and Ronny Ott had been there on Saturday night, she would know it.

He tuned his radio to a Madison rock and roll station. He loved the new music but kept that to himself. The majority of people his age thought it was the devil's music and condemned it. He loved the beat and could definitely see why all the young girls were crazy over Elvis.

He turned off Highway 60 onto T and watched for the entrance to the tavern. He made a sharp left and pulled into the parking lot. The tavern wasn't open yet, but he was sure that Mrs. Franz would be there, tidying up from the night before.

He tried the door to the entrance, found it locked, and knocked.

"We're closed," a woman called out. "Come back at eleven."

"Dottie, it's Chief Austin. I'd like to talk to you," he yelled.

A few seconds later, he heard a click and the door swung open. Mrs. Franz was standing there, a big smile on her face. "Come on in, Augie."

"I'm sorry to bother you. I just have a question or two and I'll be on my way."

"No problem. Come in and have a cup of coffee."

Austin walked into the bar and sat down. He watched as Dottie Franz poured him a cup of coffee and brought it over to the table where he was sitting. He picked it up and started to take a swallow.

"Careful," she warned. "It's hot."

"Thanks," he said and blew on the coffee to cool it down. He took a small sip and sighed. "Now, that's what I call coffee. What's your secret? This is delicious." He smiled at her and took another sip.

She looked at him and grinned. "Sorry, no secret. What can I do for you?"

"Ronny Ott seems to have gone missing. No one has seen or talked to him since Saturday. His mother told me that Pete Drollstrom and Ronny were here drinking Saturday night. Do you recall seeing them?"

Dottie Franz sat back and thought about the question. She slowly shook her head back and forth. "Nope. They weren't here."

"You're sure, Dottie? This is important."

"One hundred percent sure, Augie. I'd remember if they had been here. I shudder every time that Drollstrom boy walks through my door. He's bad news. I don't understand why you keep him on."

"It's a long story."

"It's been a while since you and Catherine have been out here for a Friday night fish fry. What's the problem? You don't like my cooking?"

"Are you kidding? You're probably the finest cook in Columbus. And, now, after this cup of coffee, you're also the greatest coffee maker person."

Dottie laughed. "Thanks. Now, you promise me that you'll bring that lovely wife of yours out here for dinner real soon."

"I will. That's a promise. Thanks for your help."

"Anytime, Augie. Anytime."

Chief Austin stared at the clock on the wall, watching the secondhand tick away the minutes. It was almost four-thirty. He had been tempted to call Pete on the radio and tell him to come in but decided that it would be better to let him finish his shift.

Jacquie was out on a call, helping get a cat out of a tree. He smiled when he thought about that phone conversation. A little four-year-old girl had called and asked for help. How fast kids grow up these days, Austin thought. Already knowing how to use a phone and not even five years old.

Austin was tempted to down a shot of whiskey before Pete showed up. He started to reach for the lower-left drawer, thought better of it, and looked up at the clock again. Just like Pete, he thought, to work late on the one day I want to talk to him.

The door to the police station was open, and from his desk, Austin could see out into the hallway. He watched as a few of the women, who worked in the mayor's office, walked by his door, noting that they were leaving early.

He heard talking in the hall, recognized Drollstrom's voice, and reached for his pack of cigarettes. He was lighting one up as Drollstrom walked in, a big grin on his face.

"I sure like dad's secretary," he declared. "Do you think she'd go out with me?"

"I haven't a clue," Austin said. "Would you mind shutting the door, Pete? I'd like to talk to you before you leave."

Pete scowled, as he pushed the door shut. "What did I do now?" he asked Austin, defensively.

"I understand that you and Ronny Ott were together Saturday night. His mom said you guys were going to meet at The Shamrock Tavern for a few drinks. I was wondering if you've talked to him since then."

Drollstrom hesitated a moment. "Nope," he told Austin. "I haven't seen him since."

"Do you have any idea where he was going after he left the tavern? And, do you remember what time it was when he left?"

Drollstrom gave him a confused look. "What's this all about? Has something happened to Ronny?"

"We don't know. So, do you know where he went?"

Pete walked over to his desk and sat down. "I haven't any idea, Chief. We had a few drinks, put our bad feelings behind us, and that was that. I figure it was probably around nine-thirty or ten when we left."

"So, you left the tavern at the same time as Ronny?"

"I did."

Austin was quiet as he stared at Drollstrom. "So, you positively met up with him Saturday night?"

"I said I did. What's going on, anyway?"

"It looks like no one has seen Ott since you and he parted ways Saturday night. It seems you're the last person he was with."

"Since Saturday? It's Wednesday today. That's four days. How could he be missing for four days and no one has said anything until now?"

"Do you know if he drove his truck out to the Shamrock?" Austin asked.

"Nah, he drove his beater. He only used his truck for work."

"His mother didn't mention that he had another vehicle."

"She might not even know about it," Drollstrom declared. "She's a nice lady, but kind of strange. Ronny didn't tell her much. He didn't want to get her all nervous."

"Why would she get nervous about him having an old car?" Austin inquired, noting that Drollstrom was using the past tense when he mentioned Ott.

"You know."

"No, I don't know. Tell me."

"He probably didn't say anything to her because she would be afraid he'd have an accident or something," Drollstrom told Austin.

"Do you think that's what happened? That he had an accident driving home from The Shamrock Tavern?"

"Well, he did have a lot to drink. That's a possibility."

"Before, you said he had a few drinks. Now, you're saying he had a lot to drink and that he might have been drunk when he left the tavern? Which is it, Pete?" Austin asked, raising his voice.

"What the hell are you yelling at me for?" Drollstrom shouted. "It's not my fault that he's missing."

"Stay there," Austin demanded, as he walked away from his desk and out the door into the hallway. He walked over to the bubbler and took a long drink of cold water. He looked at the door to the Mayor's Office and sighed. Like father, like son, he thought. He turned and walked back into the police station, slamming the door behind him.

"Before we go any further, Pete, I want you to know that I know you're lying through your teeth. I know you weren't at the Shamrock with Ott Saturday night."

Drollstrom looked away, not responding.

"I talked to Mrs. Franz. She told me you weren't there."

"Well, she's wrong. She must have forgotten," Drollstrom cried out, his face turning red.

"Where is he, Pete?"

Drollstrom didn't answer.

"Did you see Ronny Ott Saturday night or not?"

"I did," Drollstrom told him, giving Austin a dirty look. "So, what about it?"

"Where did you see him?? Austin asked.

"I went over to his house to pick him up. We were going to go have a few drinks. But, when I got there, he was acting belligerent. We had a few words and I left."

Austin stared at him. "Why in the hell did you tell me that you were at The Shamrock Tavern? Why not just tell me the truth?"

Drollstrom looked away. "Because, I wanted it to be true, okay? Ronny used to be my best friend. I wanted everyone to know that everything was okay between us again."

"Do you know how much time I've wasted because of you? Just get the hell out of my sight before I arrest you."

"For what?" Drollstrom shouted.

"For. . ." Austin caught himself before he said anything else. Right now, he didn't have enough evidence against Drollstrom to accuse him of a crime. He certainly didn't want him to know that he was a suspect in Arlis' rape and murder.

"Come on, Chief, tell me. What evidence do you have that I've done anything wrong?

Austin lit up another cigarette and stared at Drollstrom. "Just leave, will you? We're done here."

"You're crazy if you think you can arrest me," Drollstrom shouted. "Do you know who I am?"

"I don't give a flying fuck who you are," Austin interrupted.

"This isn't the end of this, Augie," Drollstrom shouted, as he walked out of the room, slamming the door behind him.

Austin opened the lower left drawer of his desk, pulled out a bottle of whiskey, opened it, and took a long swallow. "That's Chief Austin, you asshole," he whispered to himself.

Chapter Thirty-eight

"I've got them," Jacquie exclaimed excitedly, as she rushed into the police station, waving the search warrants.

"See if you can get in touch with Benny and Matt. Tell them I'll need some help today." Austin told her.

"Which one are you gonna do first?" Jacquie asked.

"I think I'll start with Pete's car. If Ott was in his car Saturday night, we might find some of his fingerprints."

"What about Arlis Upton? Her prints could be there, too." Jacquie stated.

"They could be, but I kinda doubt it. I do think, however, that we're going to find out that some of the prints you pulled off his squad car are hers. I think that's where he raped her and probably killed her."

"Shouldn't we be getting those results back pretty soon?" Jacquie inquired.

"Hopefully, today," Austin said. "Also, Jacquie, when you talk to Benny and Matt, tell them that we'll meet them out at the McNally farm at. . ." Austin glanced up at the clock. "Let's say at eleven. That will give us a couple of hours to check out Drollstrom's car."

"Do you think it will take that long?"

"It could. We want to be thorough," Austin told her.

"Do you have Pete's fingerprints on file?"

"I do. I have the prints of every officer who has

ever worked here."

"Shall we get started?" Jacquie asked.

Austin grinned. "You're really up for this, aren't you?"

"I can't wait to nail his ass."

"His car keys are on his desk. Let's go."

Officer Pete Drollstrom pulled into one of the parking spots reserved for the Columbus Police Department, saw Chief Austin and Officer Gorski standing next to his car, and let out a barrage of curse words. He jumped out of the squad car and ran over to his car. "What the fuck do you two think you're doing?" he shouted.

Jacquie glanced up at him and smiled. "Back off, Pete. We're not done here."

"What gives you the right to search my car?" he asked, looking at a pile of his belongings on the ground.

"Search warrant," Jacquie said, handing him a piece of paper.

Drollstrom stared at her. "You have a search warrant for my car? For what? You're not gonna find anything in my car," he shouted.

"We already did."

"Well, you two can kiss your jobs goodbye."

"Tell me whose fingerprints you think are on those beer cans, Pete?" Jacquie said, smirking, "Why don't you tell us and save us the work of having to compare them to Ronny Ott's? Maybe, some of the fingerprints on the dashboard might belong to Arlis Upton. And, we are extremely interested in the blood on the front seat. I'd say. . ."

"That's enough, Jacquie," Austin said. "Let's finish up here. I think we have everything."

Drollstrom watched Austin and Jacquie bag some of the items that were lying on the ground. He waited until they locked up his car, then he walked into City Hall and headed to the mayor's office.

A minute later a tow truck came around the corner and stopped in front of Drollstrom's car. The driver got out and approached Chief Austin. "Is this the car I'm supposed to take in?" he asked.

"It is. You know what department to take it to, right?" Austin asked.

"I was told to drop it off at the Forensics Department," the driver answered.

"Right." Austin stepped back and handed the driver the car keys.

Jacquie pulled in behind Chief Austin's squad car and turned off the engine. Benny and Matt were standing next to Benny's car, talking to Austin. They glanced up and waved as Jacquie got out of her squad car. "This is a first for me," she said, as she approached them.

"I think it is for all of us," Benny replied. "What are we looking for, anyway?" he asked, turning to Chief Austin.

"You see that well over there?" Austin asked, pointing. "We're gonna find out if there's a body down there."

Matt looked shocked. "Are you kidding me?" he asked. "Whose body?"

"A dead man," Austin told him. "I'm not sure who."

Benny shook his head. "I don't get it. We're looking for a dead man, but you don't know who it is, and you think he's down that well. Why would you think that? I mean, is this a missing person case? And, how the hell are we gonna find a body down there? I'm not climbing down there."

"I'm not asking you to," Austin said, grinning. "Jacquie's going to climb down."

Jacquie, looking totally surprised, backed up and gawked at Austin. "I'm gonna do what? I don't think so."

"It's perfectly safe. We'll tie a rope around you and lower you down to the bottom. The well has dried up. All I can see are rocks at the bottom. You just need. . ."

"Wait a minute," Jacquie interrupted. "How do you know there's no water down there?"

"Because I was out here yesterday and I checked it out."

"Why can't Matt or Benny do it?" Jacquie asked, looking a little pale.

"You're the lightest," Austin replied.

"This is by far the worst thing you've ever asked me to do," Jacquie complained.

"Come on, Jacquie,' Benny said, grinning. "Don't be a baby."

"Did you bring a flashlight?" she asked Austin.

"I brought a couple of them and the batteries are fresh. So, let's go do this."

"I want a raise," Jacquie whined, as she followed

the three men to the well.

Two hours later, Matt and Benny gently laid a rotting corpse on a blanket on the ground, stepped back from the body and removed the hankies from their faces.

Jacquie had already left to go to the office to phone the medical examiner, Dr. Severson.

Austin reached down and checked the man's pockets, looking for something that would identify him. "Uh-huh, I've got something," he exclaimed, as he pulled a wallet out of a pocket. He walked away from the body and checked the contents. "Here's his driver's license," he told Matt and Benny. "He's Fred Kruger from Madison."

"How long do you figure he's been down there?" Benny asked.

"I have no idea," Austin said. "Even though it's been hot, it's a lot cooler down there. Maybe a couple of weeks, but that's a guess. Doc Severson can give us a better idea when he gets here."

"What do you think he was doing out here?" Matt asked.

"And, if he has a driver's license, where's his car?" Benny observed.

"All good questions," Austin said. He looked over at the body. "All good questions," he repeated softly.

"Chief, I think you should come and take a look at this," Benny said, running towards Austin.

Austin, who was sitting in the front seat of his car, door open and feet on the ground, looked up.

"Look at what?" he asked Benny.

"We found Ronny Ott," Benny told him, almost out of breath.

"You found who?" he asked, not sure if he heard right.

"We found Ronny Ott in that barn over there. Come on. I'll show you."

Austin stood up and followed Benny to the barn.

"He's way in back," Benny told him and led Austin to an empty horse stall at the far end of the barn.

Austin looked down at the wooden floor which was partially covered with dried straw and saw Ronny Ott's body lying there. He suddenly felt sick and grabbed the wall to help steady himself.

"Are you okay, Chief?" Benny asked.

Austin shook his head yes, took a deep breath, and stepped forward into the stall. It was definitely Ronny Ott and there was no doubt what had killed him. There was a bullet hole directly between his eyes.

"I want you two to search all these buildings. See if Ott's car is anywhere on the property."

"What kind of a car is it?" Benny asked.

"It's an old beater," Austin told him. "If you find a car around here, it will most likely be his."

"Or, the John Doe's," Benny said.

"Right," Austin agreed. "I guess we're looking for two cars."

Austin turned as he heard a car horn. "That's probably Jacquie," he said. He looked down at Ott's body. "What a fucking waste." He turned and walked out of the barn.

"Severson's on his way," Jacquie said, as Austin approached her. "What were you doing in there?"

"Ronny Ott's body is in the barn. He's been shot," Austin told her.

Jacquie stared at him, not believing what she had just been told. "No way, Chief. Not Ronny Ott. That's gotta be a mistake."

"It's no mistake, Jacquie. And, I know damned well that it was Pete that shot him. This time we've got a bullet and I'll bet you anything that it will match that little pistol he carries in his ankle holster."

"If Pete did shoot Ronny with that gun, don't you think he'd get rid of it?"

"I doubt it. He thinks he's smarter than everyone else and figures no one will connect him to Ott's murder," Austin commented.

"But Ronny is on McNally's property. How can you be sure that McNally didn't shoot him and hid the body here?" Jacquie asked.

"McNally has something on Pete. I think Pete dumped Ott out here to get McNally in trouble," Austin replied. He looked up as Benny and Matt came walking towards him.

"We didn't find a car," Benny told him.

"Did you check every building?" Austin asked.

"Yep. There's no car here."

Suddenly, Jacquie walked over to her squad car and opened the door. She reached inside and removed the search warrant. "Damn!" she exclaimed, as she started reading it.

Austin glanced over at her. "Problem?" he asked.

"A big problem," Jacquie said, holding up the

warrant. "This search warrant is for the well only. The barn and the outbuildings aren't included in this warrant."

Matt looked at Austin. "What does that mean?" he asked.

"It means that we had no right to enter any of the buildings on this property. When you entered the barn, it was trespassing and it was an illegal search."

"So, are you saying that if there's trace evidence on Ronny's body, it can't be used to convict someone?"

Austin shook his head up and down. "That's exactly what I'm saying, Matt."

"But we found Ronny in there," he exclaimed. "That's not right."

"It may not be right as far as we're concerned, but it's the law."

"Well, then, let's pretend we didn't find him and get another search warrant," Benny said. "We certainly have cause now, after finding that guy in the well."

"Ya, let's do that," Matt said. "I won't say anything."

"We can't do that," Austin said. "It wouldn't be right to just let Ott lay there for another day or two while we get another warrant. Besides, it would be morally wrong."

"I can still make it to Portage before the court's close," Jacquie said, looking Austin in the eyes. "I can leave right now."

Austin pursed his lips, thinking. He walked down the rocky driveway and stopped, looking out over the countryside. He turned and walked back to the three waiting cops. "Use the siren," he told Jacquie.

Chapter Thirty-nine

"Pat McNally, I am arresting you for the murders of Fred Kruger, Debra Nelson, and Ronny Ott, plus other crimes that you have perpetrated against society. You have the right to remain silent. Anything you say can and will be used against you in a court of law. You are entitled to an attorney. If you cannot afford an attorney, one will be appointed by the courts to represent you. Do you understand what I have just told you?"

McNally took a step backward and tripped on the throw rug in front of the door. Chief Austin reached out, grabbed Pat's arm, and helped steady him.

"Thanks."

"I don't need you injuring yourself while in custody," Austin declared. "Can you walk without your cane?"

"I can if I have to. It does help, though."

"Well, you're gonna have to do without it for a while. Please put your hands behind your back," Austin said, as he reached for his handcuffs.

"You don't think I killed those people, do you?" McNally asked.

"Nope, I don't. At least, not all of them. But I do think you're guilty of insurance fraud, operating a whore house, and probably, at the least, the murder of Fred Kruger."

"Who the hell is this Fred Kruger guy? I've never even heard of him, much less killed him."

"We found him in your well, Pat. On your

220

property."

"Ya? Well, I sure as hell didn't put him there."

Austin finished cuffing McNally. "Let's go," Austin said. They had just started to walk out the door when a noise startled him. "Is there someone else in the house?" he asked McNally.

McNally didn't answer him.

"Stay there," he ordered McNally. He stepped back into the house and looked around. "I know you're in there," he yelled. "Come out. Right now!"

Sandra Peary stuck her head out of the bathroom door. "It's me, Augie. Sandra Peary. I can't come out. I'm naked," she called out.

"I'll give you thirty seconds to put some clothes on and get out here," Austin told her.

Austin glanced over a McNally, who had a big grin on his face. "This isn't funny, Pat. Why didn't you tell me she was here?"

"You didn't ask," McNally replied.

"Your thirty seconds are up, Sandra," he yelled. "Get out here or I'll come in and get you."

The bathroom door opened and Sandra, wearing extremely short shorts and a small top that barely covered her belly, strolled down the small hallway to the living room. "What are you doing with Pat?" she asked Austin, an innocent look on her face.

God, she is so beautiful, Austin thought, suddenly wondering what it would be like to get her into bed. He looked away, ashamed at what he had been thinking. "I'm arresting him, Sandra."

"What for?" she asked him.

"For the same reasons that I'm arresting you. I'm

so glad you're here. You saved me the trouble of trying to find you."

"No fucking way you're arresting me," she yelled. "I haven't done anything wrong. Tell, him, Pat. Tell him I haven't done anything wrong."

"Chief Austin, Sandra hasn't done anything wrong," McNally said, smirking.

"Sandra Peary, I am arresting you for the murders of Fred Kruger, Debra Nelson, and Rose Thomas. I am, also, arresting you for unlawful acts of prostitution. You have the right to remain silent. Anything you say can and will be used against you in a court of law. You are entitled to an attorney. If you cannot afford an attorney, one will be appointed by the courts to represent you. Do you understand what I have just told you?"

Sandra glanced over at Pat. "Pat, what's he talking about?"

Pat shrugged. "He thinks we killed some people."

"You must be fucking nuts," she yelled at Austin.

"Let's go," he said.

Sandra looked at McNally again. "Pat, what should we do?" she asked him.

"We should go with Chief Austin and try to get this straightened out."

"But we didn't do anything wrong?" she cried.

"Then, we don't have anything to be worried about," he told her.

"Karen Berke and Annie Berg, I am arresting you for the murders of Fred Kruger, Debra Nelson, and

Rose Thomas. I am, also, arresting you for unlawful acts of prostitution. You have the right to remain silent. Anything you say can and will be used against you in a court of law. You are entitled to an attorney. If you cannot afford an attorney, one will be appointed by the courts to represent you. Do you understand what I have just told you?"

"The murder of Fred who?" Annie asked. "I don't know anyone by that name."

"I need to take you both down to the station," Jacquie told them. "Is it necessary for me to cuff you?"

Annie shook her head no.

"Karen?" Jacquie inquired. "Are you going to give me any grief?"

Karen stared at her. "I don't understand," she said. "I didn't kill anyone."

"I need to take you in," Jacquie said. "Chief Austin wants to talk to you."

"But this is ridiculous," Karen said. "We didn't kill Debbie. We loved her."

"Stop talking," Annie yelled at her. "Just shut up and don't say anything."

"But, Annie. . ."

"Karen! Shut the fuck up!" Annie screamed.

"Let's go, ladies," Jacquie said.

"Can I call my mom first?" Karen asked her, tears running down her cheeks.

"You'll get to make a call at the station," Jacquie said. "Until then, I suggest you both keep your mouths shut."

Chapter Forty

Officer Pete Drollstrom looked up from his desk, wondering what all the noise in the hall was about. He stood up when he saw Karen Berke standing in the doorway, sobbing.

"Karen," he cried out, "what's the. . ."

"Sit down, Pete," Jacquie told him, as she pushed Annie Berg into the room, shoving her into Karen.

"What the hell are you doing, Jacquie?" Drollstrom yelled.

"Annie and Karen are under arrest. I'm locking them up," she told him.

Drollstrom started to say something, but a second commotion in the hallway caught his attention. He sat back down and watched as Chief Austin walked into the room with Pat McNally and Sandra Peary. His heart rate accelerated and he felt his face flush, as he realized that Pat, who was in cuffs, had been arrested.

Drollstrom kept quiet, waiting for someone to tell him what was going on. He knew if Pat had talked, he was in deep shit trouble.

Jacquie and Austin led their prisoners into the back room, which housed the three holding cells.

"I didn't do anything wrong," Karen cried out, tears running down her face.

"I'll be back to talk to you in a little while," Austin told them, as he turned to leave the room.

"Could I get a drink of water?" Sandra asked.

"I'll bring you some," Jacquie told them and walked back into the main office.

"Pete," she said, "would you mind getting some water for Sandra?"

"No, Jacquie, you get it," Austin told her. "I want to talk to Pete for a minute."

"Sure thing," Jacquie said. She grabbed one of the paper cups that they used for coffee and walked out to the bubbler in the hallway.

"Your car will be back here later today. Forensics didn't find anything substantial. I'm sorry for the inconvenience."

Drollstrom glared at Austin. "Well, I told you they wouldn't find anything," he said, a smug look on his face.

"Well, that's not exactly what I said," Austin declared. "The bloodstain on the front seat is suspicious. But you used some pretty strong cleaner on it, so getting a good sample was impossible," Austin told him.

"And, what about all those fingerprints from dead people you were so sure you were going to find?" Pete asked, sarcastically. "You were wrong there, too, weren't you?"

"Yes, I was. We didn't find any other prints in your car, except yours. However, Pete, we did find Arlis Upton's prints in the squad car you drive."

"I already told you that sometimes Sam used that car. She was never in that car with me," Drollstrom said.

Austin walked over to the table and poured himself a fresh cup of coffee. He looked over at Drollstrom, who was tapping his pencil on his desk. "We found Ronny Ott," Austin blurted out.

Drollstrom's hand jerked, making the pencil fly out of his hand and land on the floor in front of Austin.

"Whoops. Sorry. Well, that's good news," Drollstrom said. "So, where was he?"

"We found him out on McNally's farm, dead in a barn."

Drollstrom looked shocked. "That's terrible. How did he die?"

"He was shot between the eyes. He would have died instantly. The medical examiner figures he was shot late Saturday night"

"Do you have any idea why Pat killed him?"

"Who said it was McNally that killed him?"

"Well, I just put two and two together. You said that Ott was found on his property and you just locked him up." Drollstrom replied. "If you ask me, that adds up to murder.

"Are you still wearing that ankle holster?" Austin asked him.

Drollstrom hesitated, wondering where that question was coming from. "Nah," he said after a few moments. "I quit wearing that a long time ago."

"So, you don't have it on you now?" Austin asked.

"Nope."

"What kind of a gun is it?"

Drollstrom shrugged. "Why? What difference does it make?"

"I'd like to see it, that's all."

"I lost it. Anyway, if you hadn't taken my service revolver away, I never would have worn it."

"You shot Cuddles, Pete. For no good reason, if I recall," Austin said.

"He was going to bite me."

"No, he wasn't and you know it. You overreacted."

Drollstrom shook his head no. "He attacked me. I was only protecting myself."

"Cuddles might have weighed ten pounds at the most, Pete. He was the friendliest dog in Columbus. He loved everybody."

"Whatever. Anyway, don't you think it's about time you gave me my gun back?"

"Not yet," Austin said. He glanced up at the clock. "It's almost noon. Why don't you take your lunch break?"

"Aren't you gonna tell me what's going on? Why is everyone locked up?"

Austin started with Karen Berke, who he figured was the weakest of the four, planning to finish the interrogations with Pat McNally. He didn't expect their cooperation, but he did hope that one of them would eventually break down and talk. Therefore, he was shocked when Karen, who had answered his first couple of questions with 'no comment', suddenly broke down and started talking. He sat back and listened, occasionally interrupting to ask a question or to have her clarify something.

She told him that Pat McNally had run a house of ill repute out of the farmhouse. Karen explained that they did this because they all wanted to open a restaurant and needed to make some quick money.

"You know that prostitution is illegal, don't you?" he had asked her.

"I guess, but we weren't really hurting anyone," she had replied.

When Austin asked her if she knew what had happened to Debbie, Karen started sobbing. It took a while for her to regain her composure, but when she did, she disclosed the entire story. Austin fought to keep his emotions to himself, as he learned how Debbie had accidentally been murdered by a client who was into rough sex.

"I've never seen Pat so angry," she had told Austin. "The guy offered Pat money to keep quiet. He acted like it was nothing and said that Debbie was just another piece of trash that could easily be replaced. That's when Pat totally lost it. He hit that guy really hard, and as the guy fell, he hit his head against the edge of a table." Karen had looked at Austin, her cheeks wet from her tears. "It was an accident, Chief Austin. Pat didn't mean to kill him," she had said.

He felt sick to his stomach when Karen told him how sorry she was for leaving Debbie under the popcorn wagon. They never would have done it, if they hadn't been high on drugs and alcohol, she stated.

He believed Karen when she said she knew nothing about Rose's overdose, leaving Austin undecided if Rose Thomas had accidentally killed herself, committed suicide, or was murdered.

And, when he mentioned Ronny Ott to her, she gave him a blank look, obviously knowing nothing about his death.

Austin called Jacquie into the interview room. "I need to keep Karen separated from the others until I finish talking to them. There's a spare room upstairs with a couple of chairs and a table. I want you to take her up there and keep an eye on her."

"Sure thing," Jacquie said. "Come on, Karen. Let's go for a walk."

She looked at Jacquie, her eyes red from crying. "I need to use the restroom, first," she uttered softly.

Annie Berg stared at Austin, a defiant look on her face.

"I know everything, Annie. Karen told me everything."

"Then, what am I doing here?" Annie asked.

"I thought maybe you'd like to tell your version of what happened to Debbie. You might feel better if you get it off your chest."

"The only talking I'm going to do is to my attorney. I have nothing to say to you." She sat back and folded her arms across her chest.

"That's your choice," Austin said. "Right now, though, I'm not sure exactly who I'm going to be charging with what crimes. I'm sympathetic to what happened to Debbie, although the way you disposed of her body leaves a lot to be desired."

Annie looked up at him. "I'm so sorry about that. We were so out of it. We never should have done that."

"So, what about it, Annie? Is there anything you would like to tell me?"

It was almost two-thirty by the time he finished questioning Annie. He noticed that Drollstrom wasn't

229

at his desk and he wondered what he was up to. Probably getting rid of his ankle pistol, he thought. He was hungry, but he didn't want to leave the station to go get something to eat. If Catherine is home, she could make me a sandwich and bring it over, he thought. He picked up the phone and called his wife.

Sandra Peary was a lot tougher. She was defiant and would not answer any questions. Finally, she sat back in her chair and quietly said, "Lawyer." He quit questioning her and placed her back in her cell.

Catherine Austin walked into the station carrying a basket full of food. "I've got fried chicken, some biscuits, and potato salad," she stated, as she set the basket down on Austin's desk.

Austin stared at her. "All I wanted was a sandwich," he told her.

"I know and I put a couple of sandwiches in there, too. Augie, I've had a number of phone calls about the arrests you've made. I imagine everyone's hungry, so I made enough for everyone."

"This isn't a hotel, Catherine."

"They still need to eat, don't they?

Austin shook his head yes. "I guess."

"I made some lemonade, too."

Austin smiled at her. "No wonder I love you," he said, as he reached for a chicken leg. "You're always thinking of others."

He took a big bite. "This is absolutely delicious," he told her.

Chapter Forty-one

"What kind of deal will you give us if I tell you everything?" Pat McNally asked as he sat down across from Austin.

"You're joking," Austin said. "I've got enough evidence to put you and your friends away until you're old and gray."

"You really don't, Chief. I imagine Karen and Annie told you a whole bunch of stuff, but you don't have any physical evidence."

"Sorry, Pat, but I don't make deals. I have two bodies that were found on your property. I have statements that you ran a cat house. I know why Debbie was murdered. I think I have enough, Pat."

"How about I give you Pete Drollstrom? You could be rid of him forever. Then, would you consider making a deal?"

Austin sat back in the hard, wooden chair and studied McNally's face.

"I've got the bullet," Pat said, smiling.

"Let's talk."

"Can I have a glass of that lemonade?"

Austin handed McNally a glass of lemonade and sat down in a chair across from him.

"Thanks," McNally said.

"Pete shot you, didn't he?" Austin said, anxious to get started.

"He did, although to be fair, it was an accident. At least, I'm pretty sure it was. I was chasing a raccoon out of the house. . . Actually, I was shooting at

231

a raccoon that had gotten in the house. It ran out of the kitchen door and I followed, shooting at it. I came around the corner of the house and the next thing I knew, Pete was shooting at me."

"This is the farmhouse you're talking about. Right?"

"Right. When I asked him what he was doing there, he told me he was driving by, heard shots, and thought someone was in trouble. He was there to save the day," McNally said, grinning.

"Did you believe him?

"Hell, no. He'd been spying on me."

"Why would he do that?" Austin asked.

"He had heard the rumors about a whorehouse in Columbus and was trying to get proof that I was involved with it. Pete likes to know things about people in town. He uses the information to get what he wants. People are afraid of him, you know."

"I've heard that," Austin told him.

"Anyway, after he shot me, he drove me to the hospital. I kept the bullet. It came from that pistol he carries in his ankle holster. I told him he owed me a favor for not telling you that he shot me."

"And, that favor was to torch the farmhouse, so you could collect the insurance," Austin stated.

McNally looked surprised. "You know about that?"

"I do. That's insurance fraud, you know."

"I know. I was just trying to help the girls out and figured they could use a little extra money."

"Tell me about Fred Kruger."

"That's the guy you found in the well, right?"

"It is."

"Debbie had several customers who liked it rough. Debbie enjoyed it, and she liked the extra money she got for doing it. Kruger got carried away, and accidentally smothered her. Afterward, he got smart with me, acting like it was no big deal, and I hit him. He fell against the edge of a table and that was all she wrote. I didn't mean to kill him. It just happened."

"And, instead of calling for help, you threw him down the well."

McNally grinned. "It seemed like a good idea at the time."

Austin stared at him. "Do you think this is funny, Pat?"

"Sorry."

"Did you kill Ronny Ott?"

McNally shook his head and sighed. "I liked the guy. Why would I kill him?"

"Because he knew too much. Pete has a big mouth. He told Ronny about your plan to burn down the farmhouse. He told him what you were using the farmhouse for. You thought if Ott wasn't around, I wouldn't have any proof against you. You wanted him dead."

"No way!" McNally shouted, getting excited. "I had nothing to do with that. Pete wanted to get even with Ronny for decking him in that tavern."

"Did he tell you that, Pat? If you knew that Pete was out to get Ott, why didn't you say something?"

McNally hesitated, not wanting to incriminate himself. Drollstrom had told him that he was going to take care of the situation with Ott but had never said specifically what he was going to do.

"Pat? Did you know?"

"No. I knew Pete was upset with Ott, but the last I heard he was going to apologize to him."

"Did Pete ever mention Arlis Upton to you?"

McNally looked confused. "Arlis? No. Why?"

"Just checking."

"Chief Austin, Pete and I aren't friends. We don't hang out. The only reason I know anything about Pete is that we talked a little after he shot me. He loves to talk about himself. In fact, he never shuts up. But he never mentioned anything about any woman.

"So, you weren't involved in Ott's death in any way?"

"God, no! We all know that it was Pete who hid Ott's body in my barn. For god's sake, he tried to pin this on me. I had nothing to do with it."

"I need a break," Austin told him. "Do you need to use the john?"

"No, thanks. But I could use a cigarette if you can spare one."

"I'm going to weigh all the facts, Pat, but right now you're facing the following charges. The murder of Fred Kruger, the murder of the John Doe that was in the farmhouse when Pete burned it down, not reporting the death of Debbie Nelson, illegally disposing of two bodies, running a house of ill repute for personal gain, withholding evidence. . ." Austin looked at McNally. "I'm sure there's more. You're in a lot of trouble, my friend."

McNally stared at him, not believing his ears. "I

thought you were going to make a deal," he said, quietly. "I've given you everything you need to nail Drollstrom and now you're charging me with all this shit."

"Calm down. I said I was going to think this over. You have to understand that you're going to have to do some jail time. I can recommend the D.A. give you a break on the murder of Kruger and charge you with involuntary manslaughter. I believe it was an accident. The death of the bum is a different story. You. . ."

"But I didn't kill him," McNally said. "It was Drollstrom."

"You two colluded to burn the house down, and the bum was collateral damage. I think you'll be charged with voluntary manslaughter. As far as the insurance fraud goes - well, that's gonna be up to the insurance company to decide if they want to press charges. You could make a phone call and cancel the claim. I don't know if that will help, but you could try."

"Can I use your phone?" McNally asked.

Austin grinned. "Later. As far as running a whore house. . ." he hesitated. "Well, it's mostly hearsay, and with the house gone, there's no physical proof. Actually, Pat, I'm thinking you just had a lot of parties and people threw money into a pot to help cover the expenses."

McNally looked up at him, surprised.

"I'm not pursuing your side business, which will leave the girls off the hook for prostitution, but there's still the matter of dumping Debbie's body. I think they'll be charged for that, but most likely will only get probation."

McNally shook his head up and down. "Good. Thank you."

"Tell me, something, Pat."

McNally looked up at him. "What."

"Just how much of this whore house thing was Sandra's idea?"

"Between you and me?" McNally asked.

"Ya."

"All of it. She planned the whole thing and the rest of us all went along for the ride. She was obsessed with the idea of running a family restaurant here in town and wanted to make some fast money. We never expected anyone to get hurt."

"Too bad the ride got so bumpy," Austin commented.

"I guess," McNally agreed.

"Did she kill Rose?"

Pat looked surprised at the question. "Why would she have killed Rose? They were friends."

"Did she?"

"Rose had a lot of issues, Chief."

"Rose was about to talk to me. Perhaps, Sandra decided she needed to be silenced and fed her those sleeping pills."

Pat shook his head no. "No way. She would never have done that. Whatever happened to Rose was Rose's doing. Sandra had no part of it."

"Do you think Sandra's capable of murder?"

Pat smiled. "Sandra comes across as being tough, but underneath that facade is a tender-hearted woman. No, I don't think she could kill anyone," he lied.

Chief Austin sat back and lit up a cigarette. He inhaled deeply and let out the smoke. "Alright, then. I guess we're done for now," Austin said. "I'll need you to write down what you've told me. Leave out the prostitution part of it." He pushed a pad of paper and a pen over to McNally.

"What about the girls?" McNally asked.

"I'll talk to them and let them know what we agreed on."

McNally reached for the pen. "Then, I guess we have a deal."

"I'll call the County Sheriff and have you guys picked up tonight. Unfortunately, it's Friday. It looks like you'll all be spending the weekend in lock-up at the county jail. I doubt they'll be a bail hearing before Monday. You might want to call your attorney."

"What the fuck?" Why can't we stay here?"

"Sorry. No can do."

"Come on, Augie," he whined.

"Nope. Now, tell me where I can find that bullet?"

Chapter Forty-two

Chief Austin pulled his car over and parked across the street from McNally's house. "I'll be a son of a bitch," he uttered. "What the hell is he doing here?"

He exited his squad car and walked towards McNally's house, keeping his eyes focused on the open front door. He climbed the few steps that led to the front porch and opened the screen door. He entered the house and stood just inside the door, listening. He heard sounds coming from down the hallway and proceeded to walk in that direction, trying to muffle his footsteps. He stopped in front of Pat's bedroom. Officer Drollstrom, his back to Austin, was standing in front of a dresser, throwing clothes out onto the floor.

"Exactly what do you think you're doing?" Austin asked, in a loud voice.

Drollstrom jumped. He looked over his shoulder and frowned when he saw Austin standing there.

"What are you looking for, Pete?"

"I'm looking for the gun that killed Ronny. I know it's here somewhere."

Austin smirked. "You're fast with the answers. I have to give you that."

"Well, it's true," Drollstrom told him.

"I think you're looking for a bullet. The same bullet that you used to shoot Pat McNally. You do know that searching someone's home without a search warrant is against the law, don't you?"

"You mean like you did when you searched McNally's barn?" Drollstrom asked, sarcastically.

"Let's go," Austin said, ignoring his comment.

"I'm not going anywhere with you," Drollstrom told him.

"Pete, I'm arresting you for the murder of Ronny Ott."

Drollstrom looked at him and laughed. "You are so fucking out of your mind."

"There's more," Austin said. "Living room – now!"

Austin stood aside and waited for Drollstrom to walk out of the room. He followed him down the hallway to the living room.

"Sit," Austin demanded.

"I didn't kill anyone and you know it," Drollstrom muttered.

"I said sit down," Austin said and waited while Drollstrom sat down on the couch. Austin stood, towering over him, and stared down at him. "I'm also arresting you for arson and for the murder of the John Doe who was burned to death when you set McNally's farmhouse on fire."

Drollstrom looked up at him, hate written all over his face. "You've lost your mind, Augie," he said, emphasizing the name Augie.

"You are also under arrest for the rape and murder of Arlis Upton."

"You can't prove that," Drollstrom yelled.

"You think your blood type isn't going to match the fetus that died when you killed her? You raped her and when she came to you for money for an abortion, you said no. Then, when she threatened to tell Sam what you had done, you killed her."

"Wrong! It never happened. This time you've gone too far, Augie."

239

"You know what was really low, Pete?"

Drollstrom glared at him.

"When you tried to frame Sam for her death," Austin declared. "First you kill his girlfriend and then you have the balls to tell me you found his lighter by the river. You hit bottom that time. But I don't know why I'd expect anything better from you. You're just like your no-good father."

"You better watch what you say about my dad or I'll. . ."

"You'll what, you piece of shit?" Austin yelled. He glanced down at Drollstrom and grinned. "I guess I have to charge you for shooting Pat McNally, too."

"I didn't shoot Pat. He shot himself."

"No, he didn't. You did. He told me."

"That was an accident," Drollstrom yelled. "Did he tell you that?"

Austin grinned. "Why don't you just confess to everything and save us the trouble of a trial, Pete?"

Drollstrom looked away, not answering.

"No smart remarks now?"

"I didn't rape her, you know," Drollstrom said, softly. "She wanted it. I just gave her what she wanted."

"She was in love with Sam. There's no way she wanted your ugly fat body on top of her."

"You bastard," Drollstrom yelled and started reaching down towards his ankle.

"Stop!"

Drollstrom hesitated and looked up.

"Lift your pants leg, Pete."

What for?"

"I want to see if you're carrying," Austin replied.

"I'm not."

"Let me see," Austin said. "Now!"

Drollstrom reached down and pulled up his pants leg, revealing his ankle holster. "So, what if I am? What's it to you?"

"You were going for your gun, weren't you?" Austin asked, glaring at him.

"No, I wasn't."

"You were going to shoot me. I can't believe you had the balls to try that."

Pete stared at his boss. "Fuck you, Augie."

Chief Austin stared back at Pete, stepped back a few feet, slowly pulled his gun out of his holster, and aimed it at Pete.

Pete's face turned white, fear written in his eyes. "What do you think you're doing?" he asked Austin. "You know better than to aim a loaded gun at someone."

"I do know that," Austin said softly. "Unless, of course, you intend to use it."

"You're bluffing. There's no way you're gonna shoot me. Now, put that gun away or I'll have my dad fire your ass," Pete stared up at Austin. "This isn't funny, Augie."

"That's Chief Austin to you. And, you're right. It isn't funny," Austin said, as he pulled the trigger.

About the Author

I was born in Idaho in 1939. My father's job demanded that we frequently move so, by the age of ten, I had lived in Idaho, Montana, Colorado, Michigan, and finally Wisconsin.

I am the proud mother of three wonderful sons and two fantastic grandsons. I have no plans to acquire another husband, as they are just too much work.

For most of my life, I worked as an accountant. Two years before I retired, I did a complete switch in careers and managed two Curves fitness facilities in Illinois. I retired in 2002 and moved to Branson, MO. In 2012, I moved to Indiana to be closer to my family and have resided in Highland since then.

I enjoy a good laugh and figure it's my sense of humor that has kept me going when times were tough. Reading has always been one of my passions and I still read a couple of books a week.

Most of my life, I have written poems for amusement. In 2014, I wrote my first book, *Blueberries and Bears and My Brother's Shoes*, a book about growing up in the forties and fifties. After I self-published it and gave it to friends and family to read, they encouraged me to get serious about my writing.

The Mayor's Son takes place in 1957, in my old hometown of Columbus, Wisconsin. It's been sixty years since I graduated from Columbus High School and it seemed fitting to write a book that takes place back then. The characters are totally fictional, of course, and we didn't have an Officer Drollstrom on the police force. Thank God.

Crossing Sydney was my first novel and it was published in July 2015. It has received outstanding reviews.

Don't Smother Your Mother, A Bad Week in Hollister, and *Floating Face Down,* are the Sheriff "Cowboy" Berkson series. I wavered a lot about the ending the series, as I knew it meant the end of writing about some of my favorite characters. However, I figured there are a lot of other people roaming around in my head that can wind up in a book. So, I sadly said goodbye to Cowboy and the cast of characters in the three-book series.

Let's Play Autopsy, my fourth book, takes place in Kalispell, Montana. The persons and places are fictitious, although at one time in my life when I was quite young, I did live in that city.

Cowtown is my sixth mystery novel. It takes place in a made-up Chicago neighborhood. The Campanales are an unusual family, who mistakenly think they are more qualified to take care of the town bully than the cops. Never a good idea, as they soon find out in this exciting story with an unexpected ending.

Willerton Woods is my seventh mystery novel. My dad hunted in the Upper Peninsula and we made yearly trips before hunting season to spruce up his deer blind.

I never thought that, at the age of 76, I would become an author. I have set a goal for myself to write at least ten books before I die. I guess I better stick with it because you just never know.

I certainly am enjoying my retirement knowing, when I get up each morning, I have something to look forward to. You can find out more about me and my books at www.susanlpare.com. Please visit me there and feel free to send me your comments.